The
Santa Claus
Book

The Santa Claus Book

by IRENE SMITH
Pictures by HERTHA DEPPER

FRANKLIN WATTS, INC.

NEW YORK

ACKNOWLEDGMENTS

To Appleton-Century-Crofts, Inc., for "The Spirit of Christmas" by Edith Houghton Hooker, from *St. Nicholas Magazine.* Copyright, 1915, by the Century Company. Reprinted by permission of Appleton-Century-Crofts, Inc.

To the Beckley-Cardy Company, for permission to use "The Telltale" and "How Can it Be?" by Gloria Brumby, and "Probably" and "Unworthy," by Inez George Gridley, from *The Big Book of Christmas Entertainments.*

To Admiral Richard E. Byrd, for permission to use "Santa Claus at the North Pole."

To Mrs. Katherine H. Dent, for permission to use "Santa Claus and the Mouse," by Emilie Poulsson.

To Asa Don Dickinson and Ada M. Skinner, editors of *The Children's Book of Christmas Stories,* published by Doubleday, Doran & Co., Inc., for permission to use "Little Girl's Christmas," by Winnifred E. Lincoln.

To E. P. Dutton & Co., Inc., for permission to use "The Story of Santa Claus," from *Welcome Christmas!,* collected by Eleanor Graham, published and copyrighted by E. P. Dutton & Co., Inc., New York, 1932.

To Harper & Brothers, for permission to use: "Christmas at the Hollow Tree Inn," from *The Hollow Tree and Deep Woods Book,* by Albert Bigelow Paine, copyright, 1910, by Harper & Brothers, copyright, 1938, by Dora L. Paine; "The Christmas That Was Nearly Lost," from *This Way to Christmas,* by Ruth Sawyer, copyright, 1916, by Harper & Brothers, copyright, 1944, by Ruth Sawyer Durand; "Why Santa Claus Chose the Reindeer," from *The Giant Who Liked Chocolate Cake,* by Estella H. Lane, copyright, 1939, by Harper & Brothers.

To George G. Harrap & Co., Ltd., for permission to use "Christmas Eve," from *The Little White Gate,* by Florence Hoatson.

To Houghton Mifflin Co., for permission to use "Kriss Kringle," by Thomas Bailey Aldrich, and "Piccola," by Celia Thaxter.

7

To Alfred A. Knopf, Inc., for permission to use "Santa Claus Comes to America," by Caroline Singer and Cyrus Leroy Baldridge, copyright, 1942, by Alfred A. Knopf, Inc.

To Lothrop Lee & Shepard Co., New York, for permission to use "Santa Claus, a Wonder Story for Little Children," from *A Story Garden for Little Children*, by Maud Lindsay, copyright, 1913.

To The Macmillan Co., for "Before Christmas," from *The Pointed People*, by Rachel Field, copyright, 1924 and 1930, by the Macmillan Company and used with their permission.

To Stella Mead, for permission to use "On Christmas Eve," from *The Land of Never-Grow-Old*, published by George Newnes, Ltd.

To Oxford University Press, for permission to use "A Rhyme for Nicholas," from *Ten Saints*, by Eleanor Farjeon, copyright, 1936, by Oxford University Press, New York, Inc.

To Charles Scribner's Sons, for permission to use "The Mouse That Didn't Believe in Santa Claus," adapted from "The Mouse and the Moonbeam," from *A Little Book of Profitable Tales*, by Eugene Field.

To Reverend William Dana Street, for permission to use "Giant Grummer's Christmas," published by *Story Parade*.

To *The Sun*, for permission to use "Is There a Santa Claus?" By Francis P. Church.

To the Viking Press, for "Mikulas, Bearer of Gifts," from *The Good Master*, by Kate Seredy; copyright, 1935, by Kate Seredy, reprinted by permission of the Viking Press, Inc., New York.

To Mrs. Maude O. Walters, editor of *A Book of Christmas Stories for Children*, published by Dodd, Mead & Co., for permission to use "The Baby Bears' Christmas Stockings."

To my librarian friends, especially in the public libraries of Brooklyn, White Plains, and Dobbs Ferry, who located the books I needed.

I. S.

TO MY FATHER AND MOTHER
WHO GAVE US IN OUR CHILDHOOD CHRISTMASES
AN EVERLASTING MAGIC

About this book

SANTA CLAUS needs no recommendation or defense. This book was compiled because we should have more about him, in the stories that tell of Christmas. No other collection makes him its exclusive hero.

Santa Claus is one of the universal characters loved by the human race wherever he is known. Our ideas about him, about the way he looks and how he comes and what he means, are an essential part of the American heritage. The roots of these ideas however were transplanted to our country from many distant parts of the world. Here a wonderful image grew up around his name. Belief in these marvels requires no act of faith. "They speak the heart of truth."

Who can say what greater gift America has given to the children of all mankind?

Irene Smith

Contents

The
Santa Claus
Book

Santa Claus

Santa Claus

OLD SANTA CLAUS puts on his cap
  And buckles it under his chin.
He laughs and sings as he fills his sack
  And straps it over his sturdy back.
"I'll crowd all I can within,
  For girls and boys, such pretty toys—
I've dolls and drums and sugarplums
  For all little girls and boys."

Old Santa Claus has reindeer brown
  And a sleigh with silver bells.
He rides over all the roofs in town
  And stops at the chimney and rattles down
And this pleasant story tells:
  "Christmas is here, with gladsome cheer,
And here are toys for girls and boys—
  I've dolls and drums and sugarplums,
For all little girls and boys."

AUTHOR UNKNOWN

21

Santa Claus, a Wonder Story for Little Children

EVERY YEAR, on the night before Christmas, Santa Claus comes.

He rides in a sleigh drawn by tiny reindeer with bells on their harnesses.

Tinkle, tinkle, ring the bells, and trit-trot, go the little deer to carry Santa Claus over the world.

Santa Claus dresses in fur from his head to his heels. His leggings are fur, his coat is fur, and he wears a fur cap pulled down over his ears, for the winds of winter are icy cold.

O-o-o-o, sing the winds, tink, tinkle, ring the bells,

This story is taken from the book A STORY GARDEN FOR LITTLE CHILDREN *by* MAUD LINDSAY.

and trit-trot, go the little deer when Santa Claus rides over the world.

Santa Claus's beard is as white as the snow, and his cheeks are as red as apples, and his eyes are as bright as the twinkling stars that look from the sky to see him ride.

Twinkle, twinkle, shine the stars, O-o-o-o, sing the winds, tink, tinkle, ring the bells, and trit-trot, go the little deer when Santa Claus rides over the world.

Santa is old, old as the hills, but he is strong as a giant, and on his back he carries a pack, and the pack is full of toys. He has dolls and drums, and balls and tops, wagons and sleds, tea sets with blue roses painted on them, and horns with red and white stripes; and all of them are for little children. As soon as the children are asleep on Christmas Eve, Santa Claus comes to fill their stockings with good things and give them beautiful gifts. He knows just what the children want, every one of them, and he laughs for joy as he rides away.

Ha! Ha! laughs Santa Claus, twinkle, twinkle, shine the stars, O-o-o-o, sing the winds, tink, tinkle, ring the bells, and trit-trot, go the little deer when Santa Claus rides over the world.

The children never see him come. No, indeed! If he hears

so much as a laugh or a whisper in the house he stays outside till all is quiet. Why, once upon a time there was a little boy who did not want to go to bed on the night before Christmas. "I shall sit up and see Santa Claus," he said. He hung his stocking on the mantel, and sat in his mother's big rocking chair and waited, and watched, and waited; but all that he saw was a little gray mouse, though he stayed awake till everybody but his mother was in bed, and he could not keep his eyes open another minute. The last thing he saw as he went to sleep was the stocking hanging just where he had put it, and there was nothing in it; but—do you believe it?—when he waked up next morning it was full of goodies from tip to toe; and right in front of the hearth was a wagon with red wheels! "Oh, oh! Santa Claus has been here," said the little boy; and he clapped his hands, for he was happy as could be.

All the world is happy when Santa Claus comes. Trittrot, go the little deer, tink, tinkle, ring the bells, O-o-o-o, sing the winds, twinkle, twinkle, shine the stars, and ha! ha! laughs Santa Claus, as he rides over the world to fill the children's stockings, and to bring beautiful gifts.

A Rhyme for Nicholas

NICHOLAS, Saint of Children,
Loves to spend his wealth
On pretty toys for girls and boys,
Leaving them by stealth.
The wind in the chimney
Hears children call:
"Bring me this, Saint Nicholas!
Bring me that, Saint Nicholas!

A silky scarf,
A bag of sweets,
A big gold ball!"

This poem is from the book TEN SAINTS *by* ELEANOR FARJEON.

26

Nicholas, Saint of Sailors,
Children of the sea,
When their sails are torn by gales
Close at hand is he.
The wind in the rigging
Hears the sailors cry:
"Save us here, old Nicholas!
Save us there, good Nicholas!

Saint of Sailors,
Bring us safe
Home, high and dry!"

The Story of Santa Claus

YOU MUST OFTEN WONDER who Santa Claus was, and why anyone with such a queer name should be visiting you secretly at Christmas, dropping presents down the chimney for you, and never letting you see him! Santa Claus is a pet name for Saint Nicholas, and Saint Nicholas is the patron saint of children. That means that children are his special care, and that looking after them and making them happy is what he likes more than anything else in the world—or out of it!

Long, long ago there was a rich and noble couple whose only trouble was that they had no son. It was a great grief to them, and they never ceased to pray that God would, one day, give them one. At last, after they had prayed for many years, a little boy was born to them and they called

This story is from the book WELCOME CHRISTMAS *by* ELEANOR GRAHAM.

him Nicholas. Both father and mother were now very happy. They hung over the child and thought there had never been a child like him before. He was a lovely baby, too. He was good as gold. He never cried nor screamed nor refused to take his food. He slept a great deal, and when he was awake he just lay and smiled and crooned to himself.

For a few years everything went as well as could be desired, but when Nicholas was about eight years old a terrible sickness called the Plague took hold of the village and many people died of it. Among these were his own parents. They both died, and the child was left alone in the world. Poor little boy! It was not much help to him to have all his father's riches left to him then. He was very unhappy and grew very silent and shy. He was very rich, though, and among other things his father had left him three bars of solid gold. He had not any idea what they were worth nor what he should do with them.

As Nicholas grew up he remained always quiet and shy and humble, preferring always to do what he could to help people without being seen or thanked. He liked to slip money in hungry children's hands as he passed them in the streets, or to drop a coin as though by accident at a poor beggar's feet. He walked a great deal through the streets of Myra, the city in which he lived, but he spoke so rarely to anyone that few did more than glance at the tall thin young man striding along the narrow ways.

One night as he was returning home after one of his tramps he paused outside the house of a nobleman who had once been rich but was now in a sad plight. He had three daughters, this nobleman, and as Nicholas paused he heard the eldest of them say:

'Father, we have no bread left, and we are very hungry. Let us go out into the streets and beg, so that we may not starve to death.'

The old man wept and laid a hand on his daughter's head.

'My dears,' he said to them, 'wait but a little longer. Do not, I beg you, go yet into the streets to beg. Something must happen to save us from such disgrace as that. Wait but until tomorrow!'

The girls sighed, for they were very hungry indeed, but they listened to their father and did what he told them.

Nicholas went on his way, pondering upon how he might help them. It was clear to him that if he offered money the proud old man would refuse it. Besides, that was not Nicholas's way of doing things. He had reached home and was in his own room before a way out of the difficulty occurred to him. He remembered the bars of gold. They were still in the same place where his father had left them. Nicholas fetched one and without further delay set out with it. He reached the nobleman's house, and walked round it seeking for some way of getting the bar into the house without being seen himself. On the spot where he had overheard their conversation he looked up and saw a tiny window open. The window was in the very room in which the father and daughters had been sitting. They were still there. They were all very quiet, wondering how much longer they could bear to go on. Nicholas stretched up on tip-toe and dropped the bar in, *thud*, through the window. Directly it left his hand he was off, and fled back to his own house as fast as he could go.

Inside the room the noise of the falling bar of gold startled the four wretched people. They started up. The man picked it up. Felt it. Weighed it in his hand. Looked well at it. Then he turned shining eyes on his daughters.

'Gold!' he whispered, 'my daughters, God has heard our prayers.'

On the next day he took the gold bar to the money-changers and sold it for a great sum of money. There was a great deal of happiness in that household, you may be sure. Some of the money bought them food at once; some of it kept them for a long time afterwards, and some was put aside as a dowry for the eldest daughter. Nicholas, walking in the evening as was his custom, saw the change in the house and rejoiced. Very soon he saw the marriage of the eldest girl to a rich and noble lord. The dowry had settled that.

Nicholas often strayed past the house after that, and he saw sometimes the two remaining daughters with their father.

'They should have dowries, too,' he thought to himself, and made up his mind to slip the second gold bar through the little window.

Matters fell out exactly as he had planned, and he had the pleasure of seeing the second daughter's marriage also.

'Now,' said Nicholas to himself, 'I will give the third bar of gold to the father for the third girl, and then I will go forth as a priest in the service of God.'

So Nicholas gave away the third bar of gold and the same day set forth on a pilgrimage to the Holy Land, which he had long wanted to visit. When he reached Jerusalem, however, God spoke to him and told him to go back to his own country and to stay there in the crowded cities, to do his work among the poor and needy.

Nicholas did as he was told and returned at once. On the way, the ship in which he was sailing was overtaken by a terrible storm. The winds rushed and roared through the rigging. The waves rose higher and higher till it seemed as though they must sweep over the boat and sink it. Even the sailors despaired. In the midst of it Nicholas knelt down on the deck and prayed that the storm might cease. God heard him and stayed the wind and stopped the waves so that all was peaceful and calm again, and so Nicholas got safely back to his native town.

He went into the city as he had been told, and there in Myra among the poor and needy he worked quietly and humbly so that few heard of him or knew of his goodness.

Now it happened about that time that the Archbishop of Myra died. To decide upon the new one the priests all gathered together and at their meeting it was made known that one of them had had a vision in which God had said that He would give them a sign as to who the new Archbishop would be. They were all to go to the church early on a certain morning, and the first man to come in was to be chosen.

It was Nicholas's habit to rise very early in the morning and to go into the church to pray before anyone else was about. So on the morning appointed, when the priests looked for the sign, there was Nicholas, the first in the church, on his knees praying. He was aroused by the sound of their voices acclaiming him the new Archbishop. It seemed strange to the shy, thoughtful young man, but he submitted and took up his new office with all the humility and goodness he had always shown.

For a time all went well. The poor people rejoiced as they saw him in his beautiful robes, and he did not forget them. They flocked round him and told everyone of the kind things he had done in secret when he had been living among them. Sorrow soon overtook them, however, for one year the crops failed and a state of famine prevailed among them. Corn rose to such a price that few had money to buy even a little, and soon there seemed to be no corn at all, even if anyone had had money to buy it. Many of the poor people died of starvation, and Nicholas was grieved to the heart. He spent all he had, and yet he could not get food for them. One day he walked down to the harbour, and among the ships that lay there he found two that were loaded with grain. He sought out the merchants to whom they belonged, and said:

'Sell me your grain!'

The merchants shrugged their shoulders and said they regretted very much but their cargoes were already sold to merchants across the sea. They said they had no choice but to deliver them.

'Never mind that,' cried the Archbishop. 'Only sell me your corn for my poor hungry people and, I promise you, your vessels shall be as fully loaded when you arrive at your destination as they are now, lying there in the harbour.'

The merchants consulted together. They had heard stories of Nicholas, Archbishop of Myra, and they somehow believed what he said. At length they returned to him and, bowing and smiling, announced that they had decided to let Nicholas have the grain. The corn was carried ashore and the ship set sail for the land to which it should have been taken. Nicholas fed his people and, in the fulness of time, it was told throughout Myra that the merchants had found their cargoes complete, sack for sack, when they had reached their journey's end.

So from one good deed to another, Nicholas's fame grew, and with it grew the love of everyone about him, man, woman and child. He died an old white-haired man, with a long white beard. Many were the stories told of his secret kindnesses and his good work. Indeed, people have never ceased, even to this moment, to talk of him and to tell his story, for am I not now telling you about him? And are there not many whom you, yourself, know who still speak of good kind Santa Claus?

Santa Claus
Comes to America

I F YOU ARE to know about Santa Claus, I must tell you first about a Bishop who lived more than one thousand years ago in a faraway place. His name was Nicholas. A man is never a Bishop until he has lived many years, and become very wise. But little Nicholas was extraordinarily good, and extraordinarily wise. So, the extraordinary Nicholas was made a Boy Bishop, and put in charge of many churches when he was only a child.

When the Boy Bishop grew up he was most particularly fond of children. One day, a father sent his three small sons away to school. On the first night of their journey they stopped at an inn to sleep. Bishop Nicholas knew that the innkeeper was wicked. Next morning, he went to the inn.

"I have come to ask about the three small boys," he said.

From a book by CAROLINE SINGER *and* CYRUS LeROY BALDRIDGE.

"Good Bishop, they rose early and went on their journey," the innkeeper replied.

"That is strange, for I did not see them," the Bishop said. In nook and cranny the Bishop searched. No boys were found. But in a deep, dark cellar the Bishop spied three wooden tubs. He made a sign above the tubs, and out stepped the boys as whole and as lively as ever. Never again did the innkeeper hide schoolboys in tubs! Scared out of his wickedness, he was good till the end of his days.

Rich and unselfish, Bishop Nicholas was always giving gifts. But he had a quaint way of giving his gifts. Much too unselfish to want any thanks, he left them so that people found them without knowing from whom they had come. Gathering his long red robe about him and climbing to a rooftop, Bishop Nicholas once dropped a gift down the chimney of a poor man's house while all were asleep. In the morning this gift was found in the oddest of places. It was found in a stocking which had been hung up to dry before a fireplace, exactly as so many American children hang up theirs on the night before Christmas.

Now you know the story of unselfish Bishop Nicholas as it is told to thousands of children across the sea.

In many lands across the sea people have a special day

for remembering the unselfish Bishop who was most particularly fond of children. In these lands children have a fine Christmas, although, at dinner, they have no turkey, because turkey is an American bird. But it is on Saint Nicholas Day that the children are given gifts.

In some lands a Saint Nicholas comes by day to every town with a sack full of gifts on his back. He is a jolly fellow with a bushy white beard, and a Bishop's high hat, and a long red Bishop's robe. Dancing with the children, he gives away gifts until all are gone. In another land a jolly old woman comes with Saint Nicholas and is called his "wife." It is she who gives gifts to children while her jolly husband carries the sack.

But there are lands in which children never set eyes upon Saint Nicholas, no matter how long they watch or how hard they look. These children find gifts in shoes which they have put out on the night before Saint Nicholas Day, or in stockings which they have hung up, exactly as you hang up yours on the night before Christmas.

If you asked these children one of your little, little questions, you would hear that, once each year, Saint Nicholas drops gifts down chimneys as he did long ago when he was a Bishop. You would hear that Saint Nicholas rides, by night, through the sky over mountain, and hill, and river, and lake, and treetop, and housetop. But some children say that he rides a great horse. Others say that he drives a horse and rides in a farmer's cart. But in another land, children stoutly declare that he drives the smallest of small reindeer, and rides in a sleigh which makes no sound because it was built by fairies.

Of course, Saint Nicholas leaves nothing for a bad child, unless he leaves a switch with which the child is to be soundly walloped. But the unselfish Bishop never finds a bad child. For, across the sea, children become good before Saint Nicholas Day, in the same peculiar way that American children become little saints when Christmas draws near!

Although Saint Nicholas had been visiting children across the sea for hundreds and hundreds of years, he did not visit America until three hundred years ago. Then, he did not visit the United States because there were no States. America was mostly a wilderness which still belonged to the Indians who had their own holidays. The white children lived only in scattered settlements. Most were English. But in three places, they were Dutch.

One of these places was an island. It had been bought

for twenty-four dollars from Indians whom the Dutch called "Wild Men," although they were friendly. Today, this island lies beneath the skyscrapers of New York City in the State of New York. When it belonged to the Dutch, there was no New York City. There was only a little town which the Dutch called New Amsterdam. They named it for old Amsterdam, in Holland, from which they had come in sailing ships, because in those long-ago days no one had dreamed of using steam.

On the island the children lived, at first, in houses of logs and bark. But soon they were living in big houses of stone. Around the houses the Dutch planted bulbs and flower seeds, which they brought from old Amsterdam. But the flowers spread beyond the gardens. This is why so many "wild" flowers which children gather today outside of New York City, are Dutch and not really American.

The Dutch boys and girls dressed like their fathers and mothers. Of course, the boys did not smoke long clay pipes filled with mild tobacco bought from the "Wild Men," as their fathers did. But they wore long-tailed coats and wide knickerbockers. Indoors and out, the girls wore frilled caps and dresses which came to their shoes. But both boys and girls wore red, yellow, blue, or brown stockings which their mothers knit.

When schoolmasters came from old Amsterdam, the boys went to school, while the girls had a few lessons at home. People did not yet know that a girl can learn from a book as well as a boy. But the girls were busy helping their mothers, who were very particular housekeepers.

Every day the small girls helped to scrub the floors with sand to make them white—although the floors were not often dirty, because the particular mothers made the fathers and children take off their shoes when they came inside. The small girls learned to bake, and cook, and to brew medicines from Dutch plants. Sometimes, they made new medicines from American plants, which their mothers were taught to use by the "Wild Men," who hung about, and cut wood, or ran errands, but would never work in a house. The small girls learned to knit, and to sew, and to spin thread with a wheel, and to weave with a loom. Boys did none of these tasks. But sometimes, when a boy was naughty, his mother punished him by making him weave a whole yard of cloth!

Every day the small girls and their mothers polished the brass knockers on the great front doors. They cleaned the houses from bottom to top. But Dutch mothers were so pernickety that they allowed no one to use the front doors, or set foot in the clean parlors on *ordinary* days.

On ordinary days even dressed-up visitors had to come in through the back door, and sit in the kitchen. But a Dutch kitchen was big. Its wooden benches and tables were scrubbed as white as the floor. The cooking and baking were done in a fireplace which had big stone ovens on one side. This fireplace was so huge that there was room inside for a rather large man to stand up, if he ducked his head ever so little.

The Dutch settlers were very fond of cakes and candies. So, New Amsterdam was soon dotted with bakeshops. Over the door of every bakeshop were the same three Dutch words which meant "Sweet and Delicious." Over the three words was the same picture of Saint Nicholas in a Bishop's high hat, and a long red Bishop's robe!

There was a reason for this. Saint Nicholas has always been a favorite saint of the Dutch in Holland. Sailing away from old Amsterdam, the Dutch settlers saw last of all the steeple of a church which was called "The Church of Saint Nicholas." On the island they were busy building houses, and planting crops, and trading with Indians from whom they bought furs to send to Holland. But they were not too busy to build a church. They called it "The Church of Saint

Nicholas." For they said that Saint Nicholas was the protector of every person in New Amsterdam.

The protector of every person in New Amsterdam, Saint Nicholas was the protector of every baker who lived in the town. But there was another reason for his picture upon the bakeshops. The bakers were famous for baking special cakes, and making special candies, which were eaten on only one day—Saint Nicholas Day!

Several days before Saint Nicholas Day the bakeshops began to buzz and hum as the bakers made special ginger cakes, and special candies, which the Dutch gave as gifts upon Saint Nicholas Day. Made with ground almonds, the candies were called *marzipan*. In Christmas week you can often find marzipan candies in stores which are kept by Americans who have come from faraway places. But many kitchens also buzzed and hummed. For, in many houses, the girls helped their mothers bake ginger cakes and make marzipan. Whether they were bought or homemade, the cakes and candies were all shaped like the Saint Nicholas upon the bakeshop signs.

Out of doors the Dutch boys and girls wore wooden shoes which they called *klompen*. On the night before Saint Nicholas Day the small boys and girls set their wooden klompen in a row before the kitchen fireplace, whose chimney was wide enough for a man to climb up or down. Saint Nicholas did not forget the children of the settlers who remembered him. For in the morning the children found gifts, which they said had been brought by Saint Nicholas, who had ridden his great horse from Holland, across the sea, and crept down the chimneys. Sometimes a boy or girl found a switch in a shoe. But this was a Saint Nicholas joke. For beneath the switch the child always found plenty of gifts.

On Saint Nicholas Day the pernickety Dutch mothers opened their great front doors and their spotless parlors to visitors, who came and went with gifts of Saint Nicholas cakes and candies. Every cake and candy Saint Nicholas looked as if it were made of gold, as solid as that which the unselfish Bishop gave away long, long ago. For, on the night before, the boys and girls had helped to wrap them in real gold, which had come from old Amsterdam. Pounded and rolled as thin as a leaf of paper, it was called gold leaf. You have never had candies wrapped in real gold, but you have had them wrapped in the very same way in tin foil.

By hundreds and by thousands, new settlers kept on coming across the sea from many lands. But mostly they came from England. In those days the English settlers said that America belonged to England, and to them. Because there were so many, they easily took the island, and all other Dutch places, away from the Dutch. On the island the Dutch soon had thousands of English neighbors, and their island's name was changed to New York.

In England, the English had once had a Saint Nicholas Day. Then, choir boys in all the towns had elected Boy Bishops, because the unselfish Bishop, who lived long, long ago, had been a Boy Bishop when only a child. From Saint Nicholas Day until after Christmas, the Boy Bishops had been in charge of the churches like men. They had also run wild with their friends, and begged gifts from house to house.

In America, the English had Christmas like everyone else. Then, it was not a special day for giving gifts, and some English parents were so strict that they allowed their children to do nothing on Christmas Day but go to church. They had no Saint Nicholas Day. Long before any English had crossed the sea, an English king, named Henry, had put an end to Saint Nicholas Day, and to Boy Bishops, and boys running wild.

Under the English noses of their English neighbors, the

Dutch went right on having Saint Nicholas Day on the island. Under the English noses of English children, Dutch children went right on finding gifts in their shoes on the morning of Saint Nicholas Day. But there were a few other children who also put out their shoes on the night before Saint Nicholas Day. They were children whose parents came from Belgium, and were called Walloons, and children whose parents came from Norway, and were called Norwegians. The Dutch, and Walloon, and Norwegian children all put hay in their shoes. When the gifts were found, the hay was gone! The Dutch children said that it had been eaten by the great horse of Saint Nicholas. The Walloon children said that it had been eaten by the small donkey upon which he came; while the Norwegian children declared that it had been eaten by the smallest of small reindeer which Saint Nicholas drove.

Some English children began to wonder about Saint Nicholas. With all their might they wished that he would bring gifts to them. But they called him "Santa Claus." This was their English way of saying "Sinter Klaas," which was the Dutch children's name for their favorite saint.

They had no klompen, because they never wore wooden shoes. But they had stockings. Their houses had huge fireplaces with chimneys as wide as those on the houses of Dutch, or Walloon, or Norwegian children. So, some hung up their stockings. There was nothing new about this. Across the sea, in Italy, children wore no wooden shoes. For hundreds of years they had been hanging up their stockings, and finding them filled with gifts on the morning of Saint Nicholas Day. But the English children did something which must have astonished Saint Nicholas. They hung up their stockings on the night before Christmas!

They put no hay in their stockings. But they found them bulging with gifts on Christmas Day. You can be sure of that! If they had not, more and more English children would not have hung up their stockings. Then, you and other American children might never have known about Santa Claus who goes on being most particularly fond of children year after year.

On the island, and in other places, the Dutch and English became friendlier and friendlier. The Dutch never forgot Saint Nicholas. But they thought less and less about having a Saint Nicholas Day. They could share Christmas with their English friends who had no Saint Nicholas Day. Soon, English children were not the only ones who hung up stockings on the night before Christmas. No matter where their parents or grandparents had come from, other children spoke English. They talked of Santa Claus, and hung up their stockings when their English playmates did.

In time, the English in America quarreled with the English in England. They were tired of being ruled by an English king who lived so far away. When the quarrel came to an end the English in America were no longer English. All of the settlers were Americans, who were free to make their own laws, and rule themselves, and call their very own land the "United States."

By hundreds and by thousands, people kept on coming to be Americans who were free to make their own laws, and rule themselves. Because the country was so large, old settlers and new were always moving west and farther west. They moved west to the great Mississippi River. Afterwards, they moved west to the Rocky Mountains, and over the high mountains to the shore of the Pacific Ocean.

All the while more and more children were hearing about Santa Claus from their parents or playmates. More and more were hanging up stockings on the night before Christmas. They hung them up in houses on far-apart farms, and in far-apart mining camps, and lumber camps. They hung them up in little towns, and in big towns which were turning into cities, as railroads were built past the doors. But many children did not know that Santa Claus was also called Saint Nicholas. Others had never heard of him. Nothing had been printed about Santa Claus in American newspapers or books. So he had not yet become a Famous Character known to everyone, as he had been known for hundreds of years in many lands across the sea.

A little more than one hundred years ago a learned gentleman was living on the island in the City of New York, which had once been the little Dutch town of New Amsterdam with pictures of Saint Nicholas above its bakeshop doors. This learned gentleman wrote serious books and serious poems with many long words for serious grownups to read. But one year he wrote a very special poem which was not serious, and did not have very many long words. He wrote it at Christmastime when New York City was covered with snow, and filled with the jingling of bells on horses drawing sleighs, in which people got around in those days. He called his very special poem *A Visit From Saint Nicholas*. Today, we call it *A Visit From Santa Claus*.

But many people call it *The Night Before Christmas*, because those are the words with which it begins.

The learned man wrote the poem for no one but his own children to read on a certain Christmas morning when they found their stockings bulging with gifts, Somehow, the poem leaked out of his house. It reached an editor. The following Christmas, Santa Claus really began to be a Famous Character. For, then, the poem was printed in the editor's newspaper. Because so many children loved it, the poem was printed again, year after year, as Christmas drew near. Then it was printed with other poems in a book.

Hundreds of children learned the poem by heart to recite. Still, they did not know who had written their favorite poem. This was a secret. For the learned gentleman was not quite sure that he wished serious grown-ups to know that he had written a poem which was not serious, and did not have very many long words.

For nearly twenty years the secret was kept by the learned man's family. Then, tucked away between his serious poems, the Christmas poem was printed in a book with the learned gentleman's name, which was Dr. Clement

Clarke Moore. Shortly, it was printed again by itself in a little book which was easy for children to hold. In the book were the words, "A Present For Good Little Boys and Girls." This was the learned Dr. Moore's joke. He was thinking of Saint Nicholas, Sinter Klaas, Santa Claus who is supposed to leave nothing for a child who is bad. But during the many, many years that the poem had been printed again and again, no one has ever asked whether the children who loved it were good or bad.

A Visit
from Saint Nicholas

"'TWAS THE NIGHT before Christmas, when
all through the house
Not a creature was stirring, not even a mouse;
The stockings were hung by the chimney with care,
In hopes that Saint Nicholas soon would be there;
The children were nestled all snug in their beds,
While visions of sugarplums danced in their heads;
And mama in her kerchief, and I in my cap,
Had just settled our brains for a long winter's nap—
When out on the lawn there arose such a clatter,
I sprang from my bed to see what was the matter.
Away to the window I flew like a flash,
Tore open the shutters and threw up the sash.
The moon on the breast of the new-fallen snow
Gave a lustre of midday to objects below;

When what to my wondering eyes should appear,
But a miniature sleigh and eight tiny reindeer,
With a little old driver, so lively and quick
I knew in a moment it must be Saint Nick!
More rapid than eagles his coursers they came,
And he whistled and shouted and called them by name:
"Now, Dasher! now, Dancer! now, Prancer and Vixen!
On, Comet! on, Cupid! on, Donder and Blitzen!
To the top of the porch, to the top of the wall!
Now dash away, dash away, dash away all!"
As dry leaves that before the wild hurricane fly,
When they meet with an obstacle, mount to the sky,
So up to the housetop the coursers they flew,
With a sleigh full of toys—and Saint Nicholas, too.
And then in a twinkling I heard on the roof
The prancing and pawing of each little hoof.
As I drew in my head, and was turning around,
Down the chimney Saint Nicholas came with a bound.
He was dressed all in fur from his head to his foot,
And his clothes were all tarnished with ashes and soot;
A bundle of toys he had flung on his back,
And he looked like a peddler just opening his pack.
His eyes, how they twinkled! his dimples, how merry!

His cheeks were like roses, his nose like a cherry;
His droll little mouth was drawn up like a bow,
And the beard on his chin was as white as the snow.
The stump of a pipe he held tight in his teeth,
And the smoke it encircled his head like a wreath.
He had a broad face and a little round belly
That shook, when he laughed, like a bowl full of jelly.
He was chubby and plump—a right jolly old elf;
And I laughed, when I saw him, in spite of myself.
A wink of his eye and a twist of his head
Soon gave me to know I had nothing to dread.
He spoke not a word, but went straight to his work,
And filled all the stockings; then turned with a jerk,
And laying his finger aside of his nose,
And giving a nod, up the chimney he rose.
He sprang in his sleigh, to his team gave a whistle,
And away they all flew like the down of a thistle;
But I heard him exclaim, ere he drove out of sight:
"Happy Christmas to all, and to all a good-night!"

CLEMENT C. MOORE

Before
Christmas

Before Christmas

NOW NOT A window small or big
But wears a wreath or holly sprig;
Nor any shop too poor to show
Its spray of pine or mistletoe.
Now city airs are spicy sweet
With Christmas trees along each street,
Green spruce and fir whose boughs will hold
Their bright festoons and fruits of gold.
Now postmen pass in threes and fours
Like bent, blue-coated Santa Claus.
Now people hurry to and fro
With little boys and girls in tow,
And not a child but keeps some trace
Of Christmas secrets in his face.

This poem is from the book THE POINTED PEOPLE *by* RACHEL FIELD.

The Christmas that was Nearly Lost

IT WAS FOUR O'CLOCK on Christmas morning and Santa Claus was finishing his rounds just as the milkman was beginning his. Santa had been over to Holland and back again where he had filled millions of little Dutch shoes that stood outside of windows and doors; he had climbed millions of chimneys and filled millions of American stockings, not to mention the billions and trillions of Christmas trees that he had trimmed and the nurseries he had visited with toys too large for stockings. And now, just as the clock struck four, he had filled his last stocking and was crawling out of his last chimney onto the roof where the eight reindeer were pawing the snow and wagging their stumps of tails, eager to be off.

This story is from the book THIS WAY TO CHRISTMAS *by* RUTH SAWYER.

Santa Claus heaved a sigh of relief as he shook the creases out of the great magic bag that was always large enough to hold all the toys that were put into it. The bag was quite empty now, not even a gum-drop or a penny whistle was left; and Santa heaved another sigh as he tucked it under the seat of his sleigh and clambered wearily in.

"By the two horns on yonder pale-looking moon," quoth he, "I'm a worn-out old saint and I am glad Christmas is over. Why, I passed my prime some thousand years ago and any other saint would have taken to his niche in Heaven long before this." And he heaved a third sigh.

As he took up the reins and whistled to his team he looked anything but the jolly old saint he was supposed to be; and if you had searched him from top to toe, inside and out, you couldn't have found a chuckle or a laugh anywhere about him.

Away went the eight reindeer through the air, higher and higher, till houses looked like matchboxes and lakes like bowls of water; and it took them just ten minutes and ten seconds to carry Santa safely home to the North Pole. Most generally he sings a rollicking song on his homeward journey, a song about boys and toys and drums and plums, just to show how happy he is. But this year he spent the whole time grumbling all the grumbly thoughts he could think of.

"It's a pretty state of affairs when a man can't have a vacation in nearly five hundred years. Christmas every three hundred and sixty-five days and have to work three hundred and sixty-four of them to get things ready. What's more, every year the work grows harder. Have to keep up with all the scientific inventions and all the new discoveries. Who'd have thought a hundred years ago that I should have to be building toy aeroplanes and electric motors? And the girls want dolls' houses with lights and running water! I declare I'm fairly sick of the sight of a sled or a top, and dolls and drums make me shiver. I'd like to do nothing for a whole year, I tell you—nothing! It's a pretty how-d'y'do if the world can't get along for one year without a Christmas. What's to prevent my taking a vacation like any other man? Who's to prevent me?"

The reindeer had stopped outside Santa's own home and he threw the reins down with a jerk while he tried his best to look very gruff and surly.

"Suppose I try it. By the Aurora Borealis, I *will* try it!"

And then and there Santa Claus began his vacation.

He closed up his workshop, locked the door, and hung

the key in the attic. He turned his reindeer loose and told them to go south where they could get fresh grass, for he would not need them for a year and a day. Then he made himself comfortable beside his fire, and brought out all the books and the papers he had been wanting to read for the last fifty years or more, and settled down to enjoy himself. He never gave one thought to the world or what it would do without him; therefore, it never occurred to him to wonder if the news would get in the papers. But you know and I know that in time everything that happens gets into the papers; so the news spread at last all over the world that Santa Claus was taking a vacation and that there would be no Christmas next year. And what do you think happened then?

First of all the Christmas trees stopped growing. "What's the use?" they whispered one to another. "We sha'n't be wanted this year, so we needn't work to put out new shoots or keep especially green and smart-looking." And the holly and the mistletoe heard them, and they said: "Well, why should we bother, either, to get our berries ready as long as we shall not be needed for decoration? Making berries takes a lot of time, and we might just as well spend it gossiping."

Next, the storekeepers began to grumble, and each said to himself, "Well, if Christmas isn't coming this year why should I spend my time making my shop-windows gay with gifts and pretty things?" And the pastry cooks and the confectioners said they certainly would not bother making plum-puddings, Christmas pies, or candy canes.

Soon the children heard about it. For a long while they would not believe it, not until Christmastime came round again. But when they saw the Christmas trees looking so short and shabby, and the Christmas greens without their berries, and the streets quiet and dull, and the shop-windows without the pretty things in them, they grew sober and quiet, too. And in less time than I can tell you the whole world grew stuffy and stupid and silent and unlovely. Yes, the whole world!

Now, in a very small house in a very small town that stands just midway between the North Pole and the equator and half-way between the Atlantic and Pacific oceans (you can find the town for yourself on any map if you look for it with these directions) there lived a small boy. He was sturdy and strong, and he had learned two great lessons—never to be afraid and never to give up. He saw what was happening all over the world, because everybody be-

lieved that Christmas had been lost, and he said one day
to his mother:

"Mother, little Mother, I've been thinking this long while
if Santa Claus could see how things are going with everyone down here he would bring Christmas back, after all.
Let me go and tell him?"

"Boy, little boy," said his mother, "tell me first how you
will find your way there. Remember there are no signposts
along the road that leads to Santa Claus."

But the boy squared his shoulders and took a firm grip
of his pockets and said he, "Why, that's easy! I'll ask the
way and keep on till I get there."

In the end his mother let him go. As he walked along
slowly he questioned everything he passed—birds, grass,
winds, rain, rivers, trees. All these he asked the fastest
road to Santa Claus; and each in turn showed him the
way as far as he knew it. The birds flew northward, singing
for him to follow after; the grass swayed and bent and
made a beaten path for him; the river carried him safely
along its banks in the tiniest shell of a boat, while the winds
blew it to make it go faster. Each horse or donkey that he
met carried him as far as he could; and every house door
was opened wide to him, and the children shared with him

their bowls of bread-and-milk or soup. And wherever he passed, both the children and the grown-ups alike called after him, "You'll tell him; you'll make Santa Claus come and bring our Christmas back to us!"

I cannot begin to tell you the wonderful things that happened to the boy. He traveled quickly and safely, for all that it was a long road with no signposts marking the way; and just three days before Christmas he reached the North Pole and knocked at Santa Claus's front door. It was opened by Santa himself, who rubbed his eyes with wonder.

"Bless my red jacket and my fur boots!" he cried in astonishment. "If it isn't a real, live boy! How did you get here, sirrah?"

The boy told him everything in just two sentences; and when he had finished he begged Santa to change his mind and keep Christmas for the children.

"Can't do it. Don't want to. Couldn't if I did. Not a thing made. Nothing to make anything of. And you can't have Christmas without toys and sweets. Go look in that window and see for yourself." And the old saint finished quite out of breath.

The boy went over to the window Santa had pointed out

and, standing on tiptoe, peered in. There was the workshop as empty as a barn in the spring. Spiders had built their webs across the corners and mice scampered over the floors, and that was all. The boy went slowly back to Santa and his face looked very sad.

"Listen to this," he said, and he took a sea-shell from his pocket and held it close to old Santa's ear. "Can you hear anything?"

Santa listened with his forehead all puckered up and a finger against his nose.

"Humph! It sounds like somebody crying away off."

"It's the children," said the little boy, "as I heard them while I passed along the road that brought me here. And do you know why they were crying? Because there are no trees to light, no candles to burn, no stockings to hang, no carols to sing, no holly to make into wreaths—no gladness anywhere. And they are very frightened because Christmas has been lost."

Then Santa did the funniest thing. He blew his nose so hard that he blew tears into his eyes and down his cheeks.

"Fee, fi, fo, fum—I'm a stupid old fool!" said he. "It's too late to do Christmas alone this year; but I might—yes, I might—get help. The world is full of spirits who love the children as much as I do. If they will lend me a hand, this once, we might do it."

Then he went into his house and brought out his wonderful magic whistle that calls the reindeer; and he blew it once, twice, three times; and the next instant the eight were bounding over the snow toward him.

"Go!" he commanded. "Go as quickly as ever you can to all the spirits of the earth, water, and air, and tell them Santa Claus needs their help this year to bring back Christmas to the children."

Away flew the reindeer, and in less time than it takes a cloud to scud across the sky they were back again and with them the most wonderful gathering that has ever been seen since the world was made. There were giants from Norway and trolls from Sweden; there were dwarfs and elves from the mines of Cornwall and fairies from the hills of Ireland; there were brownies from Scotland and goblins from Germany; the Yule nisse and the skrattle from Denmark; and fairy godmothers from everywhere. And from the ocean came the mermaids and the mermen; and from the rivers and brooks came nixies and nymphs and swan maidens. And they all came eager to help. Santa Claus brought down from the attic the key of the workshop and soon everybody was busy at his own particular craft. Not a word was spoken, and for those three days not a soul rested or slept.

The dwarfs and the elves made hammers and planes and saws, knives and slates, trumpets and drums, rings and pins and necklaces of precious stones, for they are the oldest metal-workers under the sun. And the fairies are the finest spinners; and they spun cloth of silk, ribbons and fine laces, yes, and flaxen hair for dolls. The leprechaun, who is the fairy cobbler, made slippers of all colors and sizes from baby-dolls' shoes to real little girls' party slippers and boys' skating-boots. The giants cut down trees and sawed them into logs and boards while the trolls made them into boats and houses, sleds and beds and carriages. The mermaids gathered shells and pearls for beads; the brownies stitched and sewed and dressed the dolls that Santa himself had made. I don't know what the nixies made, unless it was the sea-foam candy.

There was one little goblin too little to know how to do anything, and as no one had time to teach him he wandered about, very unhappy, until a bright idea popped into his head. Then away he scuttled down to the timber-lands to tell the Christmas trees to hurry up and try to grow a bit, because the children would need them, after all.

Well, the long and short of it was that on Christmas Eve

everything was finished; and never since Santa Claus was a lad himself had there been such an array of toys. They were so fine and they shone so bright that the children going to bed that night said to one another, "Look up yonder and see the Northern Lights!"

The toys were at last packed in the sleigh and the boy climbed in on the seat next to Santa, and they were just driving away when a wee old Irish fairy woman stepped up with a great bundle.

"'Tis stockings," said she. "I've knitted one for every child, for I knew well the poor things would never be hanging up their own this night."

So it happened that the Christmas that was nearly lost was found, after all, and when the children woke up in the morning they saw their stockings full of toys and the tall green trees all trimmed and waiting for them. And when Santa reached the North Pole again, very tired and sleepy, but not at all grumbly, he heard a noise that sounded like running brooks and singing birds and waving grasses and blowing winds all wrapped up together; and he said to himself:

"Dear, dear me! What can that be? It sounds very like the laughter of little children all over the world."

And that is precisely what it was.

The Telltale

WELL, IT'S FUNNY, you'll admit,
That no one seems to know
Why Santa brings the very things
That we have wanted so.

When I was telling sister
That I wanted a red ball,
And she said that the only thing
She longed for was a doll,

There was a soft wind whispering
Among the trees that day.
Perhaps it was telling Santa Claus
What it had heard us say.

GLORIA BRUMBY

Why Santa Claus Chose
the Reindeer

THIS IS A STORY about the very first Christmas Eve that Santa Claus ever made his trip around the world. He was quite a young man then, and he had found it rather dreary at the North Pole, with nothing to do but slide down icebergs and play with the Polar Bears. One day, some of the Snow Birds that come north for the summer told him about many children living in the rest of the world, who were sad because they had no toys. That gave Santa Claus an idea. He built a great big work shop and called together the Elves and Brownies and Fairies, who were his good friends. All the year long, they worked together, making dolls and sleds and games and books.

This story is from the book THE GIANT WHO LIKED CHOCO-LATE CAKE *by* ESTELLA HITCHCOCK LANE.

The animals wanted to help. They, too, were Santa Claus' friends. He let them into the shop, but it just didn't work very well. The Polar Bears, who insisted on playing with the dolls, were so clumsy they were always dropping and breaking them. The Seals *would* stand up on their tails and dance to the tunes of the music boxes, and were in everybody's way. The Arctic Dogs just couldn't resist shaking up all the stuffed cats and bunnies. The Reindeer suddenly became quite frivolous when they saw all the gay balloons. They tossed them into the air with their noses, but the balloons caught on their antlers and broke with a bang.

Santa Claus finally just had to put out the animals and lock the door. They stood in the snow, looked longingly into the windows, and felt hurt because Santa Claus didn't come out to play with them any more. In fact, they grumbled a good deal.

Finally, the toys were all completed. The shop was overflowing.

Santa Claus drew a long breath and sat down to rest, while all the Elves and Brownies and Fairies curled up and went to sleep, they were so tired.

"Now," said Santa Claus, "the next question is how to

get all these things to the children! Here are the toys and there is my sleigh waiting to take them, but who will pull it?"

"We will," cried the Polar Bears, delighted at a chance to have a share in things again.

"We will!" cried the Reindeer.

"Oh, please let us!" exclaimed the Seals, flopping up to Santa and crowding around him.

"The idea!" cried the Dogs. "The very idea of Seals drawing a sleigh! They're so slow they wouldn't get there for a year. We are the ones to do it, of course."

This hurt the Seals' feelings. They were very sensitive about being so slow on land. When Santa Claus saw big tears rolling down from their eyes and dropping onto their flippers, he just couldn't stand it, for he was very tender hearted.

"Of course the Seals shall do it," he said. "What if they are a little slow? If they keep at it, they'll get there all right."

He hitched the Seals up to the sleigh, and away they went, flopping along over the ice. It was a little slow, but Santa Claus was very patient. When, however, they were about 15 degrees from the North Pole and Santa Claus told them to head first for Alaska, one Seal said:

"Oh, no! Let's go to Greenland first. I have a third cousin who lives in Greenland, and I've always wanted to see that country. This is a great chance!" And he set out for Greenland.

"I should say not!" said the second Seal. "I've always heard that the fish in the waters of Australia are the most delicious in the world. We'll go to Australia first." And he set out for Australia.

Each Seal wanted to go in a different direction. Santa Claus tried to reason with them.

"But the main thing is to get these gifts to the children. We can see every one of these countries in the end, if only you will all pull together and follow my directions."

But the Seals were very stubborn; and Santa Claus had to give up and go back to the North Pole.

"I'll let the Dogs do it," he said to himself. "After all, they are the ones best fitted to draw the sleigh."

He hitched up the Dogs and set out again. But before they had reached Alaska the Dogs began to quarrel with each other.

"You've got to pull your share of the load or I won't pull mine," said the first Dog.

"I *am* pulling my share. You're the one that's holding back," snarled the second Dog.

"I think you're all leaving most of it to me!" whined another Dog.

"Come! Come!" said Santa, "this is no way to do. Let's stop trying to see who's *not* doing his share. Let's all try to pull as hard as we can ourselves and never mind what the other Dog does. After all, the main thing is to get these gifts to the children, isn't it?"

The Dogs agreed that it was. They all wanted to get the gifts to the children, but each one was so afraid he was doing more than his share.

Finally, the first Dog stopped short. That stopped the rest of them. It stopped Santa Claus and the sleigh, too.

"I'm not going any further unless the rest will do their share," said the first Dog.

Then Santa Claus almost lost his patience.

"If you can't all forget yourselves and work together, we'll never get there," he said, and he took them back to the North Pole.

Both the Reindeer and the Polar Bears wanted very much to help, but the Reindeer, being always unselfish, gave in to the Polar Bears, and off they went.

"Now we'll surely get there," said Santa Claus to himself, for the Polar Bears were always very good natured and obliging. They trotted along merrily, Santa Claus singing lustily as they went, until they came down to the timber line.

"Oh, just wait a minute while I go and climb that tree!" said the first Polar Bear, and before Santa Claus could stop him, he was off, taking most of the team with him.

"No! No!" shouted the second Bear, "I want to explore that cave." And he set out in the other direction.

"Oh, dear!" exclaimed Santa Claus, very much discouraged. "I had forgotten how curious these Bears always are. We'll never get this job done, if they have to investigate everything they see."

He got out of the sleigh and made them all sit down in the snow, while he talked to them very seriously.

"Don't you see," he said, "that the main thing is to get these gifts to the children? We must do that whether or not we do all these other things."

The Polar Bears agreed, and promised to be good, and they went on again. But every time they came to something new, they forgot all about the children and the toys and started to investigate.

Santa Claus was pretty discouraged, when he had to turn back for the third time. As he finally set out with the Reindeer harnessed to the sleigh, he wondered if he'd have to give up the whole thing.

Before they went far, the first Reindeer said to the others, "Remember, we all want one thing more than anything else—to get these gifts to the children. So let's forget everything else we might like to do and all pull together until the job is done." And away they went like the wind.

The other animals were very cross. The Seals went and banged their heads against an iceberg. The Dogs crowded into a corner of the work shop and sulked. The Polar Bears spent their time teasing the Brownies. They tickled the Fairies and woke them up.

But because they forgot themselves and all pulled together, the Reindeer carried Santa's sleigh safely and swiftly around the world. And that's why they have been doing it ever since.

The Baby Bears'
Christmas Stockings

AUTHOR UNKNOWN

ONCE THERE WERE three little small bears who
lived by themselves in a house in the woods; not the three
bears that all the children know about, but three little
brother bears.

These three young bears were quite happy and comfortable in their warm snug cave, but still there was one
thing they lacked—Christmas was coming and they had
no stockings to hang up.

They had heard that Santa Claus never stopped at
places except where there were stockings hanging up, and
as the sweetest sweetmeats were made only at Christmas,
and to be had only from Santa Claus, and as bears love
sweetmeats better than anything else in the world, it is
not strange that these three little fellows determined to

get each of them a stocking to hang in the cave.

Every day they had hoped to find some, but at last the day before Christmas had come and they had found none. So that day they started out, all three together, determined to hunt until they found some, though it were long and far.

After leaving their own home woods, the first person they met was Mrs. Bossy Cow. She was eating a breakfast of dried grass and leaves in a sunny open place near some trees.

"Good-morning, Mrs. Bossy Cow!" said the eldest little bear. Mrs. Bossy Cow looked round at them, still chewing.

"Dearie me," said she, "if it isn't the three small bears that live by themselves in the cave! How are you, my dears? And what are you doing so far from home?"

"We're out after stockings," said the eldest little bear.

"Oh, I wouldn't eat stockings, if I were you," said Mrs. Bossy Cow. "I've tried it myself, when I was young. I ate one off a rope that it was growing on. Stockings always grow on ropes, you know. It made me ill."

"We don't want to eat them," cried the baby bears, together; and the eldest explained that they wanted them to hang up for Santa Claus.

"Well, I don't know where you can find them, and I should advise you to tell Santa Claus not to eat them either." And Mrs. Bossy Cow went on with her breakfast, and the three small bears hurried on.

They looked for vines of rope on which stockings grew but did not find any. On and on they went, until at last they saw Mr. William Goat standing on a rock.

"Please, Sir," said the eldest bear, "can you tell me where the stocking vines grow?"

"Stocking vines, indeed!" said Mr. Goat, staring down at them. "Who chased my youngest kid a week ago Monday?"

"I—did," said the youngest bear, bravely, "but I won't do it again."

"You may be sure you won't," said Mr. Goat. "And who put burs under the brush where my eldest son takes his nap?"

"I did!" said the eldest bear. "He makes faces at me and calls me names."

"And who ate the apples under my wild sweet apple tree?"

The second bear put his paws over his eyes. He was very fond of those little red-and-white apples.

"Stocking vines indeed!" said Mr. Goat, but the three bears were gone. They had crept around the corner of the rock and were hurrying away as fast as their legs would carry them.

And they went along, until they came to the pond where Mr. Frog lives.

"Perhaps the stocking vines grow under the water," said one.

"We'd best ask."

So they shouted, "Mis-tah Frog. Mis-tah Frog!"

Two bubbles came up to the top of the water, and then Mr. Frog's green nose and bottle eyes were seen among the dead reeds near the shore.

"We called to find out where we could get stockings to hang up for Santa Claus," said the second little bear.

Mr. Frog climbed out on a stone and sat down before he spoke.

"Well, my young friends," he said, "you did wisely to come to me. Stockings do not grow on vines; they grow on boys. When he comes to the pond here, a boy peels off his stockings and leaves them on the shore while he wades. But it would not be safe to take them, for a boy is a dangerous animal. He strikes when angry, and, what is even worse, he throws stones all the time."

"But if boys are so dangerous, and stockings grow on boys, how shall we get them to hang up for Santa Claus?"

"That I do not know," said the frog. "My advice is to let Santa find his own stockings, if he wants to, and for you to keep away from anything that looks like a boy."

The three little bears thanked Mr. Frog politely for his information and advice, and walked on with not very much hope left.

Chippie Squirrel spied them from a tree and cried after them, "Hello! all three. Where are you going?"

"Oh, it's Chippie," said the second bear. "We're looking for stockings and we can't find any."

"And tomorrow's Christmas," wailed the smallest bear.

The eldest bear explained:

"Mrs. Bossy Cow said that stockings grew on rope-vines, and Mr. Frog says they grow on boys. Which is wrong, do you know?"

"Neither," said Chippie. "There are two kinds; I've seen them both."

"Where?" said the little bears.

"Well," said Chippie, "I found the first kind a long way out of the woods. It was on a Monday. The vines bloom on a Monday, mostly. There were some on the ground (windfalls), and I thought I might as well bring them home to hold my winter nuts."

"Oh, Chippie, lend them to us," begged the bears, "just for one night! We'll bring them back safely!"

"What will you pay for the loan?" said Chippie.

"Anything you want," said the first.

"Whatever you like best of what we get," said the second.

"Half of what we get each," said the eldest.

"That's fair," said Chippie. "But I can't let you have them. I thought I'd bring them home, but a boy came along and I thought again, and I thought I would not!" and a moment later Chippie was laughing from the top of another tree.

The three small bears were too angry for anything, and hurried away. Christmas was due tomorrow, and Monday, when the stocking vines bloomed, was three days off. The littlest bear wanted to give up and go home; the second bear said that he didn't believe Santa Claus put anything in a bear's stocking anyhow. But the eldest bear wanted to go on a bit further, to see what was beyond the turn in the path.

They went on without much hope of finding anything, and reached the turn of the path.

Before them was a gray house, with a porch across the front, and on the porch sat a very, very old woman, knitting and rocking in a big chair. She looked up and said in a cracked voice, "How many pairs do you want?"

The little bears could hardly believe their ears.

"Just one stocking apiece!" shouted the eldest bear. "Hooray!"

The eldest bear trod on his paws, and then explained.

"Well," said the very, very old woman, "I think you can have them. So many come here for stockings that we can hardly keep them supplied; but my daughter and my daughter's daughter have each half a stocking knitted, and we can get them done by sundown. You can have them and pay in honey. You will find the jars on the kitchen shelf. One jar of honey for each stocking, and they must be here before the sun is down, or you can't have the stockings until tomorrow, and tomorrow will be too late!"

"We lock up at sundown!" piped a thin voice, and the little bears saw an old woman and a very old woman coming out of the house, bringing their chairs with them.

There was no time to lose. The little bears hastened to

the kitchen and each took a brown jar from the shelf. When they came out the three old women were sitting in a row, rocking and knitting hard, and they started on a run.

Now the three small bears were still very young, else they would have known where to look for honey. The littlest bear thought maybe it grew under the ground, but the others wouldn't listen to him. The oldest thought it grew on a tree, and the second said that a bee once told him it grew in flowers.

As there was not a flower living at that time, he pulled a bee by the leg out of the knot of a dead tree, but dropped it again very quickly, because the bee was so hot that he hopped.

The eldest bear was climbing a tree while this was going on, and in a moment called down from the top of the tree trunk:

"Here it is! It's in the tree! Come up, one of you, and help."

The second bear took his paw out of his mouth and scrambled up to his brother. Sure enough, there was honey in the hollow of the tree, but—out of reach.

The first bear started down into the hollow of the tree

head first, and the second bear held him by one foot, but
even then he could not reach far enough. At last the
littlest bear was let down, with the second bear holding his
foot, and the eldest bear holding his foot. And in this
way they reached the honey. It was hard work fighting off
the bees and getting the honey out, but they did it, and
with their brown jugs full and their stings plastered up
with mud, they started for the gray house.

It was now late in the afternoon. The sun was sinking
fast and the three little bears began to fear that they
would be too late. Two or three times they thought the
sun was gone when it was only behind the trees, and once
they lost their way. At last they came to the turn of the
path, and saw that there was only one little gleam of light
left.

"Wait a minute, wait a minute," they shouted, raced
around the turn, set their jars down and themselves too,
on the porch just as the last ray of sun left the treetops.

The heads of the three old women were thrust through
the crack of the door as they came up, but as the light
went, the door was shut and locked on the inside. And the
littlest bear sat down and cried.

The other two would have cried, too, if they had not

seen the window by the door open a little bit, and a thin wrinkled hand holding out three stockings.

As the eldest bear ran to get them, a voice from the inside said, "You weren't any too soon, but you weren't really too late, so here they are. I and my daughter and my daughter's daughter will take the honey in the morning. You will find some bread and molasses on the end of the porch." Then the window was closed and fastened.

The three small bears waved their stockings around their heads and danced for joy. Then they looked for the bread and molasses. Three more thankful bears could not have been found anywhere.

As they started on their journey back, a bird went out of its way to show them a short cut home, and before it was very late they were all three asleep in their own little cave, and their Christmas stockings were hanging at the opening in a row.

Now, this story was only to be about how the baby bears' stockings were found, but perhaps you will want to know if Santa brought them anything. So I will add that when they woke up in the morning the stockings were so full that they were stretched as wide as they could be. And in them was almost everything sweet that bears could

need. And the three little happy small bears gave sweetmeats to all their friends, but they said that naughty
Chippie Squirrel should not have a thing.

Then the littlest bear felt sorry for Chippie, and carried him five large sugared nut meats when his brothers
were not looking and each of the other two did the same
thing later on. Chippie had a good deal after all, though
he hadn't deserved it.

How Can It Be?

IF SANTA CRAWLS down chimneys
That are as black as night,
How can it be that Santa
Can keep his hair so white?

If Santa comes down chimneys
That are so very small,
How can he get down safely
With his big pack, and all?

GLORIA BRUMBY

On
Christmas Eve

On Christmas Eve

WHEN THE NIGHT goes gray and the
stars are gold,
When the bells for Christmas ring,
When the children close by the Yuletide log
Their Christmas carols sing;
In his sleigh he jumps, to the deer he calls,
Away to earth he flies,
Through the crystal stars of the Milky Way
And down the silver skies.

He is Santa Claus in a crimson gown,
with a beard so white and long;
We will sound his praise to the chimney-tops
In a rousing Christmas song.

This poem is from the book THE LAND OF NEVER-GROW-
OLD *by* STELLA MEAD.

He has glittering toys in his tinkling sleigh
For little ones on earth.
There are smiles in his eyes as he drives along;
　His cheeks are round with mirth.
He has presents packed for the grown-up folk
　With sprigs of mistletoe.
And the reindeer rush with their jingling bells—
　Ring-ting, ring-tang, ring-O!

　　He is Santa Claus in a crimson gown,
　　　With a beard so white and long;
　　We will sound his praise to the chimney-tops
　　　In a rousing Christmas song.

He will leave his deer on the snowy roof,
　And softly he will creep
To the small white beds where the children lie
　Half-smiling in their sleep.
For the children know that on Christmas Eve
　Their friend is on his way,

And they dream all night of a red-gowned man
  In a tinkling-jingling sleigh.

  He is Santa Claus in a crimson gown,
    With a beard so white and long;
  We will sound his praise to the chimney-tops
    In a rousing Christmas song.

The Spirit of Christmas

By EDITH HOUGHTON HOOKER

ONCE UPON A TIME there was an old man whose name was Mr. Grouch, and he had lived so many years that he could hardly count them. He was little, and thin, and bent over, and wrinkled, and he had a scraggly little beard and cross, snapping eyes. He used to carry a big stick that he would shake at the boys when they laughed at him, and he never had a smile for anybody. He lived all alone, with one crabbed old manservant in a vast house, and no one even dared to ring the doorbell.

One Christmas Eve I was coming down the street taking gifts around to some friends, and my mind was full of Christmas. There was a new fall of snow on the ground and the sleighbells were jingling. Even the busy shopkeepers seemed to be in the Christmas spirit. Banks of fir trees stood on the corners, and every now and then I passed some one proudly carrying home a tree over his shoulder. All of a sudden, whom should I see coming toward me but old Mr. Grouch, looking crosser than ever. He was shaking his stick at the Christmas trees and scowling at the fat turkeys, and for a moment I was half afraid to speak to him. Still it seemed too bad not to give the old man the season's greetings, so I called out as cheerily as I could,—"A Merry Christmas to you, Mr. Grouch!"

He turned on me, coming quite close and shaking his big stick in my face, so that he frightened me. "A Merry Nonsense!" he snarled, biting the words off short. "You should go home and attend to your business, not go running around wasting your own time and other people's. This Merry Christmasing is all nonsense, I tell you, fit only for children and simpletons. There's no such person as Santa Claus! It's all a myth concocted by idle folk to fool the children."

I stood quite still, rooted to the spot, in terror lest Santa Claus should see me in such bad company.

"You don't know what you're saying, Mr. Grouch!" I finally brought out. "It's wicked to deny the spirit of Christmas."

"Wicked or not wicked," he retorted, "I say it again—A Merry Nonsense to you and all your kind!"

He looked so fierce that I hastened on my way without another word, and as I turned the corner, I still heard him muttering,—"A Merry Nonsense! A Merry Nonsense!"

On he went homeward to his great dreary house, and there he found a frugal supper laid out by the old man-servant. He ate without appetite and then went upstairs. Then, after stuffing cotton in his ears and closing both the windows and the shutters to keep out the music of the bells and Christmas crackers, he climbed into his large four-poster bed, and pulling his nightcap down over his head, he went fast asleep.

How long he slept, he never knew, but suddenly he awoke hearing a strange sound. "*Plump!*" It was over near the fireplace, and there was a great rush of falling soot and plaster.

Mr. Grouch sat up quickly, scratched a match, and lighted his bedside candle. He lifted it high and scanned the room, peering out over the bedclothes like a strange gnome in his pointed nightcap. He stared at the fireplace, and there—what do you think he saw? He could scarcely believe his eyes—and yet, sure enough, it was Santa Claus, dressed all in ermine and scarlet velvet, red cheeks glow- ing from the cold, his white beard glistening with snow- flakes. There he stood chuckling softly and rubbing his hands together, the jolliest possible twinkle in his kind blue eyes.

"A Merry Christmas to you, Mr. Grouch," he said in a deep hearty voice.

Mr. Grouch trembled so that the candle wax dripped on his hand. "A Merry Christmas, Sir," he said, his voice sounding queer and squeaky.

"Now, Mr. Grouch," said Santa Claus, smiling broadly, "that doesn't sound natural from you. Why don't you say 'A Merry Nonsense'? You don't believe in Santa Claus, and I know it, and I've come here this evening to give you back your faith—as a Christmas present. Put that candle down—get out of bed and into your clothes while I count three. My reindeer will be tired waiting."

Then you should have seen Mr. Grouch scramble. He popped his thin legs into his trousers and laced up his boots with shaking fingers; then he pulled on his greatcoat and wound his long knitted muffler round his neck just as Santa Claus said Three!

"You've forgotten your hat," Santa Claus reminded him,

chuckling. And sure enough, there he stood, the funniest figure you can imagine, still with his pointed nightcap on his head. He tore off his cap and placed his old beaver in its stead just as Santa Claus gave him a great boost that sent him flying up the chimney. Santa followed close after, and Mr. Grouch could hear him puffing and panting, and digging his boots into the side of the chimney as he came up behind him.

On top of the house it was all singularly quiet and peaceful. There was snow everywhere, on all the roofs as far as the eye could reach, and above was the limitless heaven with the calm stars shining out.

Santa Claus stretched his arm toward the east. "It was there," he said, "before I was born, that the wise men saw the Star of Bethlehem." His voice was so full and deep that the old man trembled. He looked out over the great city and saw in a thousand homes the candles burning for Christmas. A group of singers, strolling by in the street, stopped and began to sing a Christmas carol. Suddenly the bells rang out from churches far and near. It was midnight; they were pealing the glad tidings.

"We must be off," said Santa Claus; "we are already late; we must be going."

Mr. Grouch noticed now for the first time a wonderful little sleigh drawn by eight reindeer harnessed in pairs together. In it lay Santa Claus's great pack, bursting with toys, and candy, and all sorts of joy for the children. One or two switches which Mr. Grouch saw sticking out on the top gave him a sense of uneasiness. "Get in, my man, get in!" commanded Santa Claus, and they leaped into the sleigh. The reindeer pawed the snow and snorted; then Santa Claus gave them the word and away they went. Over the housetops and over the trees, on—on—like a wind through the heavens. The old man clutched his hat down close on his head and shook with fear as he saw the great city glide by beneath them. Past the great houses they went and never drew rein. "They're rich there," said Santa Claus; "they have more than they need. We won't stop; they're untrue to the Spirit of Christmas."

After a time they came to a part of the town where the houses were all small and wretched-looking. "These are my boys and girls," said Santa, as he drew up on the roof of a particularly sorry-looking little dwelling. The reindeer shook their great horns and their bells jingled. The old man looked doubtfully at Santa Claus and then at the little chimney.

"Can we get down?" he asked fearfully.

"It's the size of their hearts, not the size of their chimneys, that makes the difference," answered Santa Claus. "I'll go first and you follow."

He stepped in the chimney and down he went, and then Mr. Grouch stepped in and down he went, also. The fire was out, and they found themselves in a tiny little room all cold and wintry. Two little stockings were hanging by the hearth, long and lank and empty, and in a bed near by, two little children were sleeping. They were smiling happily as they slept, dreaming of Christmas morning. Before the empty fireplace a woman was sitting, dressed all in black. She was slight and small, and around her thin shoulders she had drawn a shawl to protect herself from the cold. Here there was no holly, no wreaths in the windows, nothing at all to suggest Christmas except the unfilled stockings. The little mother had her eyes fixed on the dead ashes, and her thoughts could not have been happy, for tears were rolling down her cheeks. "Oh, the poor children!" she whispered to herself, with something very like a sob. "What will they do in the morning?" She hid her face in her hands and began to weep bitterly; and it was just at this juncture that Santa

Claus and Mr. Grouch came down the chimney.

"Her husband died two months ago," whispered Santa Claus to Mr. Grouch, "and she has nothing in the house for Christmas—no toys, no Christmas turkey, no nuts and raisins, nothing at all to fill those hungry stockings." A large tear rolled down his cheek. Mr. Grouch sniffed and looked uneasily at the sleeping children.

"Now," said Santa Claus, "watch and see what happens."

While the little widow sobbed on, he took one thing after another out of his wonderful pack—nuts, raisins, candy canes, a beautiful great doll with yellow curls and blue eyes that went to sleep, a little railway train, a top, a small tea set, a doll's chair, and finally, several pieces of nice warm clothing. Then he proceeded to fill the stockings with remarkable speed. When they were finished, the doll was peeping out of one, and the little engine out of the other. Mr. Grouch thought it was all over; but no, Santa Claus reached far down into his pack once more and brought out a beautiful Christmas basket. The fat legs of a turkey were standing out amid cranberries, and sweet potatoes, and oranges, and apples, and every other sort of good thing you can imagine.

Santa Claus placed the basket under the stockings, and then poked Mr. Grouch in the ribs so hard that it made him jump. "Now," said he, "watch; for she'll be looking up."

And sure enough, in a moment the little widow sighed and raised her eyes. Then you should have been there to see her. Her poor little face grew quite pink with joy, she gasped, and her breath came fast with bewilderment. She rubbed her eyes with her thin hands; she couldn't believe it was not a dream. Then she gave a little cry, just between a sob and a laugh, and fell on her knees before the basket.

She poked the fat turkey and felt deftly between all the other things until she knew exactly what was in the basket. "We'll have a beautiful Christmas dinner, after all," she said, "even a turkey!" She didn't take a thing out of the stockings—just peeped in and felt softly down the long knobby legs. "I'll leave them for the children just as he packed them, the dear saint!" she murmured to herself. She went over to the children and kissed each one softly; they smiled and wriggled cosily in their sleep. Then she looked over again at the wonderful hearthside—it seemed to Mr. Grouch that she looked straight at him, though of course she couldn't see him as both he and Santa Claus had on caps of darkness. Her face was shining with a wonderful light of love and joy. Her eyes beamed like two stars, and the room seemed to be filled with a kind of glory. "It's the blessed spirit of Christmas," she whispered brokenly, "come to cheer my fatherless little ones and me." Then she knelt down by her little bed, and it was plain that she was praying.

Santa Claus nodded triumphantly at Mr. Grouch, shaking off another big tear, and Mr. Grouch returned the look tremulously. He drew a large red handkerchief out of his pocket and wiped both eyes before speaking.

"Couldn't we take off our caps of darkness," he finally whispered, "and wish her a Merry Christmas?"

"A Merry Nonsense!" said Santa Claus, laughing until his fat sides shook. "No—we're not allowed to be seen. 'Sh-h! it's time to go up the chimney."

Up they went into the dark night where the reindeer were waiting for them. Into the sleigh they jumped and off they started, and, as the wind whistled by them, Mr. Grouch said: "Santa Claus, I feel I owe you an apology. When I saw her face—"

Santa Claus interrupted him: "If you're ready to admit

you were wrong, go out tomorrow and wish every one a Merry Christmas."

Far, far away they went, out over the rolling sea till they came to a ship which had had to sail out from port just three days before Christmas. Down into the forecastle they went, where the sailors were sadly thinking of their homes, and spread cheer around until each man wished the other a Merry Christmas.

All the long night they sped over the great world leaving joy behind them. They visited the children's hospitals, where little boys and girls were lying awake, weeping for their mothers, and they quieted them and touched them with joy, and they slept, forgetful of their pain and sorrow. They visited sinful men in prison and softened their hearts, and they stopped at the homes of the rich and bade them remember their poorer brothers.

It was a night to dream of, such as no one else but Santa Claus can ever know again, but at last the pink glow of morning showed in the eastern sky.

"It's time to be getting home," said Santa Claus. "We can be seen if we're out when the day is dawning."

In a moment they had landed safely on Mr. Grouch's roof.

"Good-by," said Santa Claus, as he politely helped his passenger to alight and to shake off the snow and start down the chimney, "and remember, you are never to say you don't believe in Santa Claus again!"

"Never in all this world!" said Mr. Grouch, in heartfelt tones. "Long live the spirit of Christmas!" He took off his hat and bowed in an old-fashioned, ceremonious manner just before the reindeer leaped into the air and started in the direction of the North Pole.

Mr. Grouch must have slid down the chimney and gone to bed after that, but in the morning he had forgotten all about that part of the adventure.

When the sun was high, the old manservant knocked at the door and reminded him that breakfast was waiting. Mr. Grouch woke with a start. "A Merry Christmas to you, Andrew," he shouted.

The old servant ran almost all the way downstairs with never a word. He thought his master must be mad, for he had never heard him give that greeting before in all his thirty years of service.

On Christmas morning I went out to take some toys to the crippled children's hospital, and there, coming down the street, whom should I see but old Mr. Grouch, a gayly decorated little Christmas tree over his shoulder, the pockets of his greatcoat bulging with toys and candy, and behind him, trooping merrily along, an endless chain of boys and girls, each with a toy and a bag of candy.

I stood stock-still with surprise and waited for the procession to come up.

"A Merry Christmas to you!" shouted Mr. Grouch, his face glowing from the crisp air, and all the children called out too, "A Merry Christmas!"

"We're going to take this tree to some fatherless children," he said. "Would you like to come along with us?"

When I found my voice, I explained my errand and, quick as a wink, Mr. Grouch said they would stop at the hospital too, on the way to the other children. So on we went, all together, and everybody smiled and beamed and echoed our joy as soon as they saw us.

It must have been merely my imagination, but Mr. Grouch's voice sounded to me just like Santa Claus's as he wished everybody "Merry Christmas!"

He spent the whole day going round from one poor family to another, taking them toys and good cheer and leaving joy everywhere behind him.

Now the most curious part of the story is yet to come.

for, would you believe it, Mr. Grouch has grown quite fat and jolly as time has gone by, until now, if you saw him, except for his black coat you would think he was Santa Claus. He has round red cheeks and a shining white beard, and his eyes are no longer cross and snapping; they beam upon every one the whole year round as if they were always saying, "I wish you a Merry Christmas!"

All of which goes to prove that Santa Claus is just as real as we think him, for each one of us can show by our own deeds and words the reality of the Spirit of Christmas.

Mister Skip

By IRENE SMITH

MISTER SKIP LIVED IN the bell tower of a crumbling old stone church. Each autumn the wind carried a few dry leaves in through the open portals of his lodging, heaping the pile already there. As these were never swept out, and as many years had passed since Mister Skip first came to live in the steeple above the hamlet of Elsenborg, he now had a snug warm bed under which to lie when the winter winds blew cold. There among his leaves, where the rusty iron bell hung high over the church, he dwelt in great contentment.

No one knew how long ago Mister Skip had got his name, because he was by far the oldest inhabitant of Elsenborg. The title was an affectionate one, for Mister Skip was a friendly little brownie. Though he enjoyed a good prank now and then and was too clever and quick to be caught in it, he was also too neighborly to do harm.

Sometimes when the children were gathering nuts in the woods and a nut dropped from the tree right into their pail, they would look up to the leafy branches and say, quite as a matter of course, "Thank you, Mister Skip."

He had a whole bag of tricks, such as hanging a blossom over the cow's ear, or sticking a leaf in the butter tub. He loved to tangle the wash on the line and roll an apple across the floor, but these jokes only made folks laugh and say, "That Mister Skip!"

His friends were not acquainted with all his tricks, however, for he kept his really important affairs to himself. He had never let anyone suspect that he was a trusted helper to old Santa Claus and that Christmas Eve was his big, busy night of the year. When all the children were in bed on the night before Christmas it was Mister Skip's duty to look into every window and see that they were sound asleep, for Santa Claus would not come near Elsenborg until Mister Skip said everything was all right.

The little brownie took this job seriously and worked hard at it. He knew each child in the village as well as the very bed in which the child slept, and never once had Mister Skip made a mistake. When he reported that the hamlet of Elsenborg was ready, Santa Claus knew that not one eyelid would be fluttering nor a single child waiting to peep. No indeed, the children could not fool Mister Skip. He had had too much experience.

To do all that he had to do on Christmas Eve, however, Mister Skip needed a partner to his plan, for brownies cannot fly and his messages to Santa Claus required the speed of wings. So he had persuaded a friend of his, a very respectable old gull, to move up from the ocean cliffs and take lodging in the bell tower. The bird had brought seaweed from his former home to build a nest beneath the ancient stone ledge, near the top of the winding stairs, and close by Mister Skip's leaf pile. These two were constant companions, so it was natural that the brownie should rely upon his bird neighbor on Christmas Eve. The gull's large grey wings were strong and swift, and furthermore he loved the excitement.

Mister Skip was able to lay out his plans quite privately, for it was many years since any outsider had invaded their steeple. When the sexton rang the church bell he just pulled the rope that hung down from the tower, and he had let ivy grow unchecked among the broken stones of the old round stairway up to the bell. The brownie and his friend the gull greatly admired the ringing music of the bell, and listened proudly when it swung back and forth on Sabbath mornings, calling the people to church. Through all the years, Mister Skip had never tired of hearing its deep tones peal out over Elsenborg. Without them he might sometimes have felt lonely in his lofty nook near the bell's wide mouth.

One year when Christmas Eve came around as usual Mister Skip and the gull had of course arranged their program with their regular care. Lamps were just lighted in the houses below when the brownie hopped down the tower stairs and through the church entry to the little street. He did not want to miss a moment of the Christmas Eve happiness in the homes of his friends.

Peeping into windows up and down the way, Mister Skip watched each family eat its supper. The children were getting ready for bed. Then came the time that the brownie enjoyed most. They were hanging up their stockings for Santa Claus. Mister Skip darted from house to house as fast as he could move and clambered upon window sills in breathless excitement, to see everything the children did. If any of them had looked closely they might have spied a small brown face, framed in frost patterns on their windowpanes, or pressed tightly against the glass.

Mister Skip fairly twitched with delight as he watched the children's shining faces and listened to their excited voices. He wriggled and grinned each time another empty stocking was placed by a chimney ready for the visit of Santa Claus. Meanwhile the gull circled overhead, watching the distant sky.

Soon the children were being tucked into bed to sleep till Christmas morning. Then Mister Skip waited impatiently until the fathers and mothers went to bed too. Finally there was not one light burning in a single house in Elsenborg.

The gull swooped down from the sky and lighted on a window sill beside Mister Skip. Both peered into a dark bedroom together.

"Are they all asleep here?" hissed the gull.

"Yes," said Mister Skip. "This makes fourteen houses that are ready. Have you seen Santa Claus yet?"

"He passed north of here a few minutes ago, and circled west. The reindeer were running like the wind."

"Keep an eye on his direction," said Mister Skip, "and come back for me when I have been to the last house." Away flew the gull and Mister Skip hurried busily to the next house down the street.

About that same time young Waldemar Nissen, lying in his deep feather bed, was saying to himself, "I shan't go to sleep, I shan't, I shan't." For days he had been planning in his own secret mind to lie awake on Christmas Eve. When he heard the reindeer stop on the roof he was going to slip softly out of bed and hide near the chimney, in time to see Santa Claus climb down with his pack. Waldemar supposed that he would not dare speak, for he was rather a timid boy; but at least he meant to find out, once and for all, what really happened in the night before Christmas.

When Mister Skip came around to peep inside the room where the Nissens slept, he knew at a glance that trouble was there. "Waldemar is as wide awake as I am this minute," groaned the little brownie to himself. "It may be an hour before he forgets and falls asleep. There's no use waiting here. I shall finish up the rest and then come back."

So Mister Skip went to each Elsenborg house that had a child living in it and to some he went two or three times before he saw that every boy and every girl was sound asleep. At last he knew that he had only one more to worry about, Waldemar Nissen, and back he scurried to take another look at him. Waldemar had his elbows in his pillow and his chin propped in his hands. "I shan't go to sleep, not for all the world. I'm not even sleepy," Mister Skip heard his whisper.

Just then the gull flew down and landed on the window sill where the anxious brownie sat. "Is something wrong here? It's getting late and we should be off."

"I know it," sighed Mister Skip, "but Waldemar thinks he is going to stay awake all night. What can we do to make him sleepy?"

The gull could not think of a thing and walked up and down outside the window flapping his wings impatiently. This waiting was a hateful business. He longed to be off across the dark night clouds with Mister Skip on his back, flying west toward where the Santa Claus sleigh had disappeared a short time before. How long must they delay!

That question worried Mister Skip even more than it did the gull. He rocked back and forth on Waldemar's window ledge, his face drawn up in a tight knot as he puzzled over how to make the boy go to sleep. What would Santa Claus say! He had never been as late as this with his message that Elsenborg was ready.

Then the brownie had an idea. He had often seen mothers rocking their babies to sleep, and he knew what they did. "Can you sing?" he whispered to the gull hopefully.

"Certainly," replied the old fellow, more ruffled than ever. "Why?"

"Because I want you to sing Waldemar to sleep. I have heard mothers' lullabies."

"What shall I sing?"

"Dear me, any song you know."

Rather pleased, the gull opened his beak and let out three hearty cries. Waldemar sat straight up in bed and stared at the window. Even Papa Nissen turned in his sleep, nearly awakened by the noise. The brownie and bird could not be seen in the darkness, but they saw plainly enough that the gull's song had the wrong effect upon Waldemar. If he had been a bit drowsy before he was startled out of it now. Both of the watchers outside were in complete despair.

"Perhaps we should go and tell Santa Claus what has happened," decided Mister Skip. "He will think Elsenborg has forgotten about Christmas."

The suggestion suited the gull, for it meant action. Mister Skip settled himself upon the bird's back, crooked his feet beneath the powerful wings, and they took off with a silent upward sweep.

The crisp air made Mister Skip tingle as they flew swiftly on. The two traveled well together. Presently they sighted Santa Claus on the outskirts of a not far distant city. He recognized them the moment the gull glided over his sleigh.

"Well, well, well!" cried the old saint. "Here you are at last. Off we go to Elsenborg."

"No, no, wait, sir," interrupted Mister Skip. "I have to tell you—I'm sorry—but Waldemar Nissen won't go to sleep."

"What!" exclaimed Santa Claus. "Two o'clock in the morning and that child not asleep?"

"Yes, sir," said Mister Skip meekly. "Can you tell me, please, what will make him sleepy?"

"Well, let me think," murmured Santa Claus. "What makes you sleepy, Mister Skip?"

"Oh, lots of things, but most of all the wind. In the winter when it blows through the bell tower and rustles the dry leaves I am sleepy. And in the summer out in the fields I hear it ripple through the tall grass and stir the little brook, and then I just fall down and close my eyes."

"Stop!" exclaimed Santa Claus. "You will put me to sleep! Now then, do you know old Granny Gruekin in Elsenborg?"

"Of course, sir."

"Do you remember that bamboo stick she leans upon when she walks about?"

"Yes, Santa Claus."

"You must borrow that stick tonight. It is hollow inside, so that when you blow through it, you will make those sounds of the wind. Take it to Waldemar's room and play for him the sleepiest wind tunes you remember."

"All right, Santa Claus. Thank you. We must hurry as fast as we can."

And straight back to Elsenborg the gull flew. Granny Gruekin lived alone near the edge of the village. Mister Skip disliked going into her house, for she was a cross old woman whom all the children feared. But he certainly was not afraid of her and boldly let himself inside her door. Noiselessly he entered the room where the old granny lay snoring in her bed. Against the footpost stood the bamboo walking stick, ready for her to put her hand upon when she wished to arise.

"I must return this before daylight," thought Mister Skip. "Granny cannot get out of bed if she has no cane to lean upon."

The brownie and gull managed between them to get the bamboo stick down the street to Waldemar's house and up to his bedroom window.

"Perhaps he has fallen asleep by now," suggested the bird, but Mister Skip shook his head. He could see the boy's wide eyes in the darkness.

"Nothing's happened yet," Waldemar was saying to himself, "but I shan't give up, I shan't. I'm only a tiny bit sleepy."

Mister Skip settled himself in the open window and raised the hollow stick to his mouth as if it were a flute. He did not know how to play the tunes of the wind that would make Waldemar sleep, but he trusted in the wisdom of Santa Claus.

Thinking how a June breeze whirs over the grasses, Mister Skip began to blow into the bamboo stick, and the stick made the tune for Waldemar. Its music was so gentle you hardly knew it was there, but the boy dimly listened. He heard green leaves waving in the sunshine and felt himself walking through a field on a golden summer's day. Remembering the warm joyous hours—drifting—half dreaming—he began to forget that Santa Claus must come tonight.

Mister Skip was soon lost in his own lullaby, playing with all his heart the wind songs he had heard. There was the autumn tune that sends the red and yellow leaves dancing down from the trees and makes the brown ones flutter along the streets of Elsenborg. Then Mister Skip played the song of the north wind as it rattles the bare branches and howls down the chimney and blows through the bell tower of the old stone church. By some good grace Mister Skip, who knew nothing about music, had for a little while on this early Christmas morning been a real musician, and the beautiful lullaby he played on Granny Gruekin's bamboo cane had made Waldemar go fast asleep.

Time was so short now for Santa's visit to Elsenborg that Mister Skip did not dare take time to return the granny's cane. The gull had him on his back in the wink of an eye and away they sailed at top speed. They were just in time too, for Santa Claus had reached the end of his journey, save only for Elsenborg.

Their important message delivered at last, the tired

brownie and sleepy gull rushed back ahead of the sleigh to pick up the bamboo stick on Waldemar's window ledge. A few minutes later it stood again by Granny Gruekin's bedside, just as usual.

Santa Claus made fast work of his visit to Elsenborg. Since it was his last stop, he unloaded his bag of every toy left in it, and the children's stockings, including the one belonging to Waldemar who had caused all the trouble, were filled full.

Up in the church tower the little brownie and the old gull were just settling down after the night's excitement when Santa Claus passed by on his way home. He drove alongside their steeple to leave a present for his two friends. Chuckling behind his beard, he stuck a sprig of holly in the gull's nest and another among the brownie's dry leaves. Then he left them each a piece of marzipan, their favorite candy, and waving good night, dashed away out of sight.

There, in the wintry sunrise, Mister Skip and the gull sat munching their delicious marzipan. Before they had finished they heard the sexton come into the church below. He was ready to ring the steeple bell and awaken Elsenborg for Christmas morning. Snatching a holly twig and sticking it jauntily in his cap, Mister Skip leaped up and caught hold of the old iron bell. As it swung back and forth he rode with it, laughing at his prank. The sexton wondered why the bell rang so loudly that morning. No one knew that Mister Skip with all his might was helping it to chime out,

"Ding dong, ding dong, dong-dong-dong!
Mer-ry Christ-mas El-sen-borg!
Mer-ry Christ-mas ev-'ry-one!"

Kriss Kringle

JUST AS THE MOON was fading amid her misty rings,
And every stocking was stuffed with childhood's precious
    things,
Old Kriss Kringle looked around, and saw on the elm tree
    bough,
High-hung, an oriole's nest, silent and empty now.
"Quite like a stocking," he laughed, "pinned up there on
    the tree!
Little I thought the birds expected a present from me!"
Then old Kriss Kringle, who loves a joke as well as the best,
Dropped a handful of flakes in the oriole's empty nest.

THOMAS BAILEY ALDRICH

124

Little Girl's Christmas

By WINNIFRED E. LINCOLN

IT WAS CHRISTMAS EVE, and Little Girl had just hung up her stocking by the fireplace—right where it would be all ready for Santa when he slipped down the chimney. She knew he was coming, because—well, because it was Christmas Eve, and because he always had come to leave gifts for her on all the other Christmas Eves that she could remember, and because she had seen his pictures everywhere down town that afternoon when she was out with Mother.

Still, she wasn't *just* satisfied. 'Way down in her heart she was a little uncertain—you see, when you have never really and truly seen a person with your very own eyes, it's hard to feel as if you exactly believed in him—even though that person always has left beautiful gifts for you every time he has come.

"Oh, he'll come," said Little Girl; "I just know he will

be here before morning, but somehow I wish——"

"Well, what do you wish?" said a Tiny Voice close by her—so close that Little Girl fairly jumped when she heard it.

"Why, I wish I could *see* Santa myself. I'd just like to go and see his house and his workshop, and ride in his sleigh, and know Mrs. Santa—'twould be such fun, and then I'd *know* for sure."

"Why don't you go, then?" said Tiny Voice. "It's easy enough. Just try on these Shoes, and take this Light in your hand, and you'll find your way all right."

So Little Girl looked down on the hearth, and there were two cunning little Shoes side by side, and a little Spark of a Light close to them—just as if they were all made out of one of the glowing coals of the wood-fire. Such cunning Shoes as they were—Little Girl could hardly wait to pull off her slippers and try them on. They looked as if they were too small, but they weren't—they fitted exactly right, and just as Little Girl had put them both on and had taken the Light in her hand, along came a little Breath of Wind, and away she went up the chimney, along with ever so many other little Sparks, past the Soot Fairies, and out into the Open Air, where Jack Frost and the Star

Beams were all busy at work making the world look pretty for Christmas.

Away went Little Girl—Two Shoes, Bright Light and all—higher and higher, until she looked like a wee bit of a star up in the sky. It was the funniest thing, but she seemed to know the way perfectly, and didn't have to stop to make inquiries anywhere. You see it was a straight road all the way, and when one doesn't have to think about turning to the right or the left, it makes things very much easier. Pretty soon Little Girl noticed that there was a bright light all around her—oh, a very bright light—and right away something down in her heart began to make her feel very happy indeed. She didn't know that the Christmas spirits and little Christmas fairies were all around her and even right inside her, because she couldn't see a single one of them, even though her eyes were very bright and could usually see a great deal.

But that was just it, and Little Girl felt as if she wanted to laugh and sing and be glad. It made her remember the Sick Boy who lived next door, and she said to herself that she would carry him one of her prettiest picture-books in the morning, so that he could have something to make him happy all day. By and by, when the bright light all around her had grown very, very much brighter, Little Girl saw a path right in front of her, all straight and trim, leading up a hill to a big, big house with ever and ever so many windows in it. When she had gone just a bit nearer, she saw candles in every window, red and green and yellow ones, and every one burning brightly, so Little Girl knew right away that these were Christmas Candles to light her on her journey, and make the way clear for her, and something told her that this was Santa's house, and that pretty soon she would perhaps see Santa himself.

Just as she neared the steps and before she could possibly have had time to ring the bell, the door opened— opened of itself as wide as could be—and there stood— not Santa himself—don't think it—but a funny Little Man with slender little legs and a roly-poly stomach which shook every now and then when he laughed. You would have known right away, just as Little Girl knew, that he was a very happy little man, and you would have guessed right away, too, that the reason he was so roly-poly was because he laughed and chuckled and smiled all the time —for it's only sour, cross folks who are thin and skimpy. Quick as a wink, he pulled off his little peaked red cap, smiled the broadest kind of a smile, and said, "Merry Christmas! Merry Christmas! Come in! Come in!"

So in went Little Girl, holding fast to Little Man's hand, and when she was really inside there was the jolliest, reddest fire all glowing and snapping, and there were Little Man and all his brothers and sisters, who said their names were "Merry Christmas," and "Good Cheer," and ever so many other jolly-sounding things, and there were such a lot of them that Little Girl just knew she never could count them, no matter how long she tried.

All around her were bundles and boxes and piles of toys and games, and Little Girl knew that these were all ready and waiting to be loaded into Santa's big sleigh for his reindeer to whirl them away over cloud-tops and snowdrifts to the little people down below who had left their stockings all ready for him. Pretty soon all the little Good Cheer brothers began to hurry and bustle and carry out the bundles as fast as they could to the steps where Little Girl could hear the jingling bells and the stamping of hoofs. So Little Girl picked up some bundles and skipped along too, for she wanted to help a bit herself —it's no fun whatever at Christmas unless you can help, you know—and there in the yard stood the *biggest* sleigh that Little Girl had ever seen, and the reindeer were all stamping and prancing and jingling the bells on their harnesses, because they were so eager to be on their way to the Earth once more.

She could hardly wait for Santa to come, and just as she had begun to wonder where he was, the door opened again and out came a whole forest of Christmas trees, at least it looked just as if a whole forest had started out for a walk somewhere, but a second glance showed Little Girl that there were thousands of Christmas sprites, and that each one carried a tree or a big Christmas wreath on his back. Behind them all, she could hear some one laughing loudly, and talking in a big, jovial voice that sounded as if he were good friends with the whole world.

And straightaway she knew that Santa himself was coming. Little Girl's heart went pit-a-pat for a minute while she wondered if Santa would notice her, but she didn't have to wonder long, for he spied her at once and said:

"Bless my soul! Who's this and where did you come from?"

Little Girl thought perhaps she might be afraid to answer him, but she wasn't one bit afraid. You see, he had such a kind little twinkle in his eyes that she felt happy right away as she replied, "Oh, I'm Little Girl, and I wanted so much to see Santa that I just came, and here I am!"

"Ho, ho, ho, ho, ho!" laughed Santa, "and here you are! Wanted to see Santa, did you, and so you came! Now that's very nice, and it's too bad I'm in such a hurry, for we should like nothing better than to show you about and give you a real good time. But you see it is quarter of twelve now, and I must be on my way at once, else I'll never reach that first chimney-top by midnight. I'd call Mrs. Santa and ask her to get you some supper, but she is busy finishing dolls' clothes which must be done before morning, and I guess we'd better not bother her. Is there anything that you would like, Little Girl?" and good old Santa put his big warm hand on Little Girl's curls and she felt its warmth and kindness clear down to her very heart. You see, my dears, that even though Santa was in such a great hurry, he wasn't too busy to stop and make some one happy for a minute, even if it was some one no bigger than Little Girl.

So she smiled back into Santa's face and said: "Oh, Santa, if I could *only* ride down to Earth with you behind those splendid reindeer! I'd love to go. Won't you *please* take me? I'm so small that I won't take up much room on the seat, and I'll keep very still and not bother one bit!"

Then Santa laughed, *such* a laugh, big and loud and rollicking, and he said, "Wants a ride, does she? Well, well, shall we take her, Little Elves? Shall we take her, Little Fairies? Shall we take her, Good Reindeer?"

And all the Little Elves hopped and skipped and brought Little Girl a sprig of holly; and all the Little Fairies bowed and smiled and brought her a bit of mistletoe; and all the Good Reindeer jingled their bells loudly, which meant, "Oh, yes! let's take her! She's a good Little Girl! Let her ride!" And before Little Girl could even think, she found herself all tucked up in the big fur robes beside Santa, and away they went, right out into the air, over the clouds, through the Milky Way, and right under the very handle of the Big Dipper, on, on, toward the Earthland, whose lights Little Girl began to see twinkling away down below her. Presently she felt the runners scrape upon something, and she knew they must be on some one's roof, and that Santa would slip down some one's chimney in a minute.

How she wanted to go, too! You see, if you had never been down a chimney and seen Santa fill up the stockings, you would want to go quite as much as Little Girl did, now, wouldn't you? So, just as Little Girl was wishing as hard as ever she could wish, she heard a Tiny Voice say, "Hold tight to his arm! Hold tight to his arm!" So she held Santa's arm tight and close, and he shouldered his pack, never thinking that it was heavier than usual, and with a bound and a slide, there they were, Santa, Little Girl, pack and all, right in the middle of a room where there was a fireplace and stockings all hung up for Santa to fill.

Just then Santa noticed Little Girl. He had forgotten all about her for a minute, and he was very much surprised to find that she had come, too. "Bless my soul!" he said. "Where did you come from, Little Girl? and how in the world can we both get back up that chimney again? It's easy enough to slide down, but it's quite another matter to climb up again!" and Santa looked real worried. But Little Girl was beginning to feel very tired by this time, for she had had a very exciting evening, so she said, "Oh, never mind me, Santa. I've had such a good time, and I'd just as soon stay here awhile as not. I believe I'll curl up on his hearth-rug a few minutes and have a little nap, for it looks as warm and cozy as our own hearth-rug at home, and—why, it *is* our own hearth and it's my own nursery, for there is Teddy Bear in his chair where I leave him every night, and there's Bunny Cat curled up on his cushion in the corner."

And Little Girl turned to thank Santa and say good-bye to him, but either he had gone very quickly, or else she had fallen asleep very quickly—she never could tell which —for the next thing she knew, Daddy was holding her in his arms and was saying, "What is my Little Girl doing here? She must go to bed, for it's Christmas Eve, and old Santa won't come if he thinks there are any little folks about."

But Little Girl knew better than that, and when she began to tell him all about it, and how the Christmas fairies had welcomed her, and how Santa had given her such a fine ride, Daddy laughed and laughed, and said, "You've been dreaming, Little Girl, you've been dreaming."

But Little Girl knew better than that, too, for there on the hearth was the little Black Coal, which had given her Two Shoes and Bright Light, and tight in her hand she held a holly berry which one of the Christmas Sprites had placed there. More than all that, there she was on the hearth-rug itself, just as Santa had left her, and that was the best proof of all.

The trouble was, Daddy himself had never been a Little Girl, so she couldn't tell anything about it, but we know she hadn't been dreaming, now, don't we, my dears?

The Mouse that Didn't Believe in Santa Claus

THE CLOCK STOOD, of course, in the corner; a moonbeam floated idly on the floor, and a little mauve mouse came from the hole in the chimney corner and frisked and scampered in the light of the moonbeam upon the floor. The little mauve mouse was particularly merry; sometimes she danced upon two legs and sometimes upon four legs, but always very daintily and always very merrily.

"Ah, me," sighed the old clock, "how different mice are nowadays from the mice we used to have in the old times! Now there was your grandma, Mistress Velvetpaw, and

This story is from the book A LITTLE BOOK OF PROFITABLE TALES *by* EUGENE FIELD.

there was your grandpa, Master Sniffwhisker—how grave and dignified they were! Many a night have I seen them dancing upon the carpet below me, but always that stately minuet and never that crazy frisking which you are executing now, to my surprise—yes, and to my horror, too!"

"But why shouldn't I be merry?" asked the little mauve mouse. "Tomorrow is Christmas, and this is Christmas Eve."

"So it is," said the old clock. "I had really forgotten all about it. But, tell me, what is Christmas to you, little Miss Mauve Mouse?"

"A great deal to me!" cried the little mauve mouse. "I have been very good for a very long time; I have not used any bad words, nor have I gnawed any holes, nor have I stolen any canary seed, nor have I worried my mother by running behind the flour barrel where that horrid trap is set. In fact, I have been so good that I'm very sure Santa Claus will bring me something very pretty."

This seemed to amuse the old clock mightily; in fact, the old clock fell to laughing so heartily that in an unguarded moment she struck twelve instead of ten, which was exceedingly careless.

"Why, you silly little mauve mouse," said the old clock,

"you don't believe in Santa Claus, do you?"

"Of course I do," answered the mauve mouse. "Believe in Santa Claus? Why shouldn't I? Didn't Santa Claus bring me a beautiful butter cracker last Christmas, and a lovely gingersnap, and a delicious rind of cheese, and—lots of things? I should be very ungrateful if I did *not* believe in Santa Claus, and I certainly shall not disbelieve in him at the very moment when I am expecting him to arrive with a bundle of goodies for me.

"I once had a little sister," continued the little mauve mouse, "who did not believe in Santa Claus, and the very thought of the fate that befell her makes my blood run cold and my whiskers stand on end. She died before I was born, but my mother has told me all about her. Her name was Squeaknibble, and she was in stature one of those long, low, rangey mice that are seldom found in well-stocked pantries. Mother says that Squeaknibble took after our ancestors who came from New England, and seemed to inherit many ancestral traits, the most conspicuous of which was a disposition to sneer at some of the most respected dogmas in mousedom. From her very infancy she doubted, for example, the widely accepted theory that the moon was composed of green cheese; and this heresy was the first intimation her parents had of her sceptical turn of mind. Of course, her parents were vastly annoyed, for they saw that this youthful scepticism would lead to serious, if not fatal, consequences. Yet all in vain did they reason and plead with their headstrong and heretical child.

"For a long time Squeaknibble would not believe that there was any such archfiend as a cat; but she came to be convinced one memorable night, on which occasion she lost two inches of her beautiful tail, and received so terrible a fright that for fully an hour afterward her little heart beat so violently as to lift her off her feet and bump her head against the top of our domestic hole. The cat that deprived my sister of so large a percentage of her tail was the same ogress that nowadays steals into this room, crouches treacherously behind the sofa, and feigns to be asleep, hoping, forsooth, that some of us, heedless of her hated presence, will venture within reach of her claws. So enraged was this ferocious monster at the escape of my sister that she ground her fangs viciously together, and vowed to take no pleasure in life until she held in her devouring jaws the innocent little mouse which belonged to the mangled bit of tail she even then clutched in her remorseless claws."

"Yes," said the old clock, "now that you recall the

incident, I recollect it well. I was here then, and I remember that I laughed at the cat and chided her for her awkwardness. My reproaches irritated her; she told me that a clock's duty was to run itself down, *not* to be depreciating the merits of others! Yes, I recall the time; that cat's tongue is fully as sharp as her claws."

"Be that as it may," said the little mauve mouse, "it is a matter of history, and therefore beyond dispute, that from that very moment the cat pined for Squeaknibble's life; it seemed as if that one little two-inch taste of Squeaknibble's tail had filled the cat with a consuming appetite for the rest of Squeaknibble. So the cat waited and watched and hunted and schemed and devised and did everything possible for a cat—a cruel cat—to do in order to gain her murderous ends.

"One night—one fatal Christmas Eve—our mother had undressed the children for bed, and was urging upon them to go to sleep earlier than usual, since she fully expected that Santa Claus would bring each of them something very nice before morning. Thereupon the little dears whisked their cunning tails, pricked up their beautiful ears, and began telling one another what they hoped Santa Claus would bring. One asked for a slice of Roquefort, another for Swiss, another for Brick, and a fourth for Edam; one expressed a preference for Cream cheese, while another hoped for Camembert. There were fourteen little ones then, and consequently there were diverse opinions as to the kind of gift which Santa Claus should best bring; still there was, as you can readily understand, an enthusiastic agreement upon this point, namely, that the gift should be cheese of some brand or other.

" 'My dears,' said our mother, 'we should be content with whatsoever Santa Claus bestows, so long as it is cheese, disjoined from all traps whatsoever, unmixed with Paris green, and free from glass, strychnine, and other harmful ingredients. As for myself, I shall be satisfied with a cut of nice, fresh American cheese. So run away to your dreams now, that Santa may find you sleeping.'

"The children obeyed—all but Squeaknibble. 'Let the others think what they please,' said she, 'but *I* don't believe in Santa Claus. I'm not going to bed, either. I'm going to creep out of this dark hole and have a quiet romp, all by myself, in the moonlight.' Oh, what a vain, foolish, wicked little mouse was Squeaknibble! But I will not reproach the dead; her punishment came all too swiftly. Now listen: who do you suppose overheard her talking so disrespectfully of Santa Claus?"

"Why, Santa Claus himself," said the old clock.

"Oh, no," answered the little mauve mouse. "It was that wicked, murderous cat! Just as Satan lurks and lies in wait for bad children, so does the cruel cat lurk and lie in wait for naughty little mice. And you can depend upon it that, when that awful cat heard Squeaknibble speak so disrespectfully of Santa Claus, her wicked eyes glowed with joy, her sharp teeth watered, and her bristling fur emitted electric sparks as big as peas. Then what did that bloody monster do but scuttle as fast as she could into Dear-my-Soul's room, leap up into Dear-my-Soul's crib, and walk off with the pretty little white muff which Dear-my-Soul used to wear when she went for a visit to the little girl in the next block! What upon earth did the horrid old cat want with Dear-my-Soul's pretty little white muff? Ah, the ingenuity of that cat! Listen.

"In the first place," resumed the little mauve mouse, after a pause that showed the depth of her emotion, "in the first place, that wretched cat dressed herself up in that pretty little white muff, by which you are to understand that she crawled through the muff just so far as to leave her four cruel legs at liberty."

"Yes, I understand," said the old clock.

"Then she put on the boy doll's cap," said the little mauve mouse, "and when she was arrayed in the boy doll's

142

fur cap and Dear-my-Soul's pretty little white muff, of course she didn't look like a cruel cat at all. But whom did she look like?"

"Like the boy doll," suggested the old clock.

"No, no!" cried the little mauve mouse.

"Like Dear-my-Soul?" asked the old clock.

"How stupid you are!" exclaimed the little mauve mouse. "Why, she looked like Santa Claus, of course!"

"Oh, yes; I see," said the old clock. "Now I begin to be interested; go on."

"Alas!" sighed the little mauve mouse, "not much remains to be told; but there is more of my story left than there was of Squeaknibble when that horrid cat crawled out of that miserable disguise. You are to understand that, contrary to her mother's warning, Squeaknibble issued from the friendly hole in the chimney corner, and gamboled about over this very carpet, and, I dare say, in this very moonlight.

"Right merrily was Squeaknibble gamboling," continued the little mauve mouse, "and she had just turned a double somersault without the use of what remained of her tail, when, all of a sudden, she beheld, looming up like a monster ghost, a figure all in white fur! Oh, how frightened she was, and how her little heart did beat! 'Purr,

143

purr-r-r,' said the ghost in white fur. 'Oh, please don't hurt me!' pleaded Squeaknibble. 'No; I'll not hurt you,' said the ghost in white fur; 'I'm Santa Claus, and I've brought you a beautiful piece of savory old cheese, you dear little mousie, you.' Poor Squeaknibble was deceived; a sceptic all her life, she was at last befooled by the most fatal of frauds. 'How good of you!' said Squeaknibble. 'I didn't believe there was a Santa Claus, and—' but before she could say more she was seized by two sharp, cruel claws that conveyed her crushed body to the murderous mouth of the cat. I can dwell no longer upon this harrowing scene. Before the morrow's sun rose upon the spot where that tragedy had been enacted, poor Squeaknibble passed to that bourne to which two inches of her beautiful tail had preceded her by the space of three weeks to a day. As for Santa Claus, when he came that Christmas Eve, bringing cheese and goodies for the other little mice, he heard with sorrow of Squeaknibble's fate; and ere he departed he said that in all his experience he had never known of a mouse or a child that had prospered after once saying he didn't believe in Santa Claus."

Santa Claus and
the Mouse

ONE CHRISTMAS EVE, when Santa Claus
  Came to a certain house,
To fill the children's stockings there
  He found a little mouse.

"A merry Christmas, little friend,"
  Said Santa, good and kind.
"The same to you, sir," said the mouse·
  "I thought you wouldn't mind

"If I should stay awake tonight
  And watch you for a while."
"You're very welcome, little mouse,"
  Said Santa with a smile.

And then he filled the stockings up
  Before the mouse could wink—
From toe to top, from top to toe,
  There wasn't left a chink.

"Now, they won't hold another thing,"
  Said Santa Claus, with pride.
A twinkle came in mouse's eyes,
  But humbly he replied:

"It's not polite to contradict—
  Your pardon I implore—
But in the fullest stocking there
  I could put one thing more."

"Oh, ho!" laughed Santa, "silly mouse!
  Don't I know how to pack?
By filling stockings all these years,
  I should have learned the knack."

And then he took the stocking down
  From where it hung so high,
And said: "Now put in one thing more;
  I give you leave to try."

The mousie chuckled to himself,
 And then he softly stole
Right to the stocking's crowded toe
 And gnawed a little hole!

"Now, if you please, good Santa Claus,
 I've put in one thing more;
For you will own that little hole
 Was not in there before."

How Santa did laugh and laugh!
 And then he gaily spoke:
"Well! you shall have a Christmas cheese
 For that nice little joke."

If you don't think this story true,
 Why! I can show to you
The *very stocking* with the hole
 The little mouse gnawed through.

EMILIE POULSSON

Probably

I DIDN'T MEAN TO close my eyes;
When Santa came I thought I'd rise
And hide down where the lights were dim,
And get a real good look at him.
But the Sandman came along too quick;
He probably works for old Saint Nick!

INEZ GEORGE GRIDLEY

Christmas at the
Hollow Tree Inn

ONCE UPON A TIME, when the Robin, and Turtle, and Squirrel, and Jack Rabbit had all gone home for the winter, nobody was left in the Hollow Tree except the 'Coon and the 'Possum and the old black Crow. Of course the others used to come back and visit them pretty often, and Mr. Dog, too, now that he had got to be good friends with all the Deep Woods people, and they thought a great deal of him when they got to know him better. Mr. Dog told them a lot of things they had never heard of before, things that he had learned at Mr. Man's house, and maybe that's one reason why they got to liking him so well.

This story is from the book THE HOLLOW TREE AND DEEP WOODS BOOK *by* ALBERT BIGELOW PAINE.

He told them about Santa Claus, for one thing, and how the old fellow came down the chimney on Christmas Eve to bring presents to Mr. Man and his children, who always hung up their stockings for them, and Mr. Dog said that once he had hung up his stocking too, and got a nice bone in it that was so good he had buried and dug it up again as much as six times before spring. He said that Santa Claus always came to Mr. Man's house, and that whenever the children hung up their stockings they were always sure to get something in them.

Well, the Hollow Tree people had never heard of Santa Claus. They knew about Christmas, of course, because everybody, even the cows and sheep, know about that; but they had never heard of Santa Claus. You see, Santa Claus only comes to Mr. Man's house, and they didn't know that either, so they thought if they just hung up their stockings he'd come there, too, and that's what they made up their minds to do. They talked about it a great deal together, and Mr. 'Possum looked over all his stockings to pick out the biggest one he had, and Mr. Crow he made himself a new pair on purpose. Mr. 'Coon said he never knew Mr. Crow to make himself such big stockings before, and Mr. Crow said he was getting old and needed things bigger, and when he loaned one of his new stockings to Mr. 'Coon, Mr. 'Coon said, "That's so," and that he guessed they were about right after all.

They didn't tell anybody about it at first, but by and by they told Mr. Dog what they were going to do, and when Mr. Dog heard it he wanted to laugh right out. You see, he knew Santa Claus never went anywhere except to Mr. Man's house, and he thought it would be a great joke on the Hollow Tree people when they hung up their stockings and didn't get anything.

But by and by Mr. Dog thought about something else. He thought it would be too bad, too, for them to be disappointed that way. You see, Mr. Dog liked them all now, and when he had thought about that a minute he made up his mind to do something. And this is what it was—he made up his mind to play Santa Claus!

He knew just how Santa Claus looked, 'cause he'd seen lots of pictures at Mr. Man's house, and he thought it would be great fun to dress up that way and take a bag of presents to the Hollow Tree while they were all asleep and fill up the stockings of the 'Coon and 'Possum and the old black Crow. But first he had to be sure of some way of getting in, so he said to them he didn't see how they could expect

Santa Claus, their chimneys were so small; and Mr. Crow said they could leave their latchstrings out downstairs, which was just what Mr. Dog wanted. Then they said they were going to have all the folks that had spent the summer with them over for Christmas dinner and to see the presents they had got in their stockings. They told Mr. Dog to drop over, too, if he could get away; and Mr. Dog said he would, and went off laughing to himself and ran all the way home because he felt so pleased at what he was going to do.

Well, he had to work pretty hard, I tell you, to get things ready. It wasn't so hard to get the presents as it was to rig up his Santa Claus dress. He found some long wool out in Mr. Man's barn for his white whiskers, and he put some that wasn't so long on the edges of his overcoat and boot tops and around an old hat he had. Then he borrowed a big sack he found out there, too, and fixed it up to swing over his back, just as he had seen Santa Claus do in the pictures. He had a lot of nice things to take along. Three tender nice chickens he had borrowed from Mr. Man, for one thing, and then he bought some new neckties for the Hollow Tree folks all around, and a big striped candy cane for each one, because candy canes always looked well sticking out of a stocking. Besides all that, he had a new pipe for each and a package of tobacco. You see, Mr. Dog lived with Mr. Man, and didn't ever have to buy much for himself, so he always saved his money. He had even more things than that, but I can't remember just now what they were; and when he started out, all dressed up like Santa Claus, I tell you his bag was pretty heavy, and he almost wished before he got there that he hadn't started with quite so much.

It got heavier and heavier all the way, and he was glad enough to get there and find the latchstring out. He set his bag down to rest a minute before climbing the stairs, and then opened the doors softly and listened. He didn't hear a thing except Mr. Crow and Mr. 'Coon and Mr. 'Possum breathing pretty low, and he knew that they might wake up any minute, and he wouldn't have been caught there in the midst of things for a good deal. So he slipped up just as easy as anything, and when he got up in the big parlor room he almost had to laugh right out, for there were the stockings sure enough, all hung up in a row, and a card with the name on it over each one telling whom it belonged to.

Then he listened again, and all at once he jumped and held his breath, for he heard Mr. 'Possum say something. But Mr. 'Possum was only talking in his sleep, and saying,

"I'll take another piece, please," and Mr. Dog knew he was dreaming about the mince pies he'd had for supper.

So, then he opened his bag and filled the stockings. He put in mixed candy and nuts and little things first, and then the pipes and tobacco and candy canes, so they'd show at the top, and hung a nice dressed chicken outside. I tell you they looked fine! It almost made Mr. Dog wish he had a stocking of his own there to fill, and he forgot all about them waking up, and sat down in a chair to look at the stockings. It was a nice rocking chair, and over in a dark corner where they wouldn't be apt to see him, even if one of them did wake up and stick his head out of his room, so Mr. Dog felt pretty safe now, anyway. He rocked softly, and looked and looked at the nice stockings, and thought how pleased they'd be in the morning, and how tired he was. You've heard about people being as tired as a dog; and that's just how Mr. Dog felt. He was so tired he didn't feel a bit like starting home, and by and by—he never did know how it happened—but by and by Mr. Dog went sound asleep right there in his chair, with all his Santa Claus clothes on.

And there he sat with his empty bag in his hand and the nice full stockings in front of him all night long. Even when it came morning and began to get light Mr. Dog didn't know it; he just slept right on, he was that tired. Then pretty soon the door of Mr. 'Possum's room opened and he poked out his head. And just then the door of Mr. 'Coon's room opened and he poked out his head. Then the door of the old black Crow's room opened and out poked his head. They all looked toward the stockings, and they didn't see Mr. Dog, or even each other, at all. They saw their stockings, though, and Mr. 'Coon said all at once:

"Oh, there's something in my stocking!"

And then Mr. Crow says:

"Oh, there's something in my stocking, too!"

And Mr. 'Possum says:

"Oh, there's something in all our stockings!"

And with that they gave a great hurrah together, and rushed out and grabbed their stockings and turned around just in time to see Mr. Dog jump right straight up out of his chair, for he did not know where he was the least bit in the world.

"Oh, there's Santa Claus himself!" they all shouted together, and made a rush for their rooms, for they were scared almost to death. But it all dawned on Mr. Dog in a second, and he commenced to laugh and hurrah to think what a joke it was on everybody. And when they heard Mr. Dog laugh they knew him right away, and they all came up and looked at him, and he had to tell just what he'd done and everything; so they emptied out their stockings on the floor and ate some of the presents and looked at the others, until they almost forgot about breakfast, just as children do on Christmas morning.

Then Mr. Crow said, all at once, that he'd make a little coffee, and that Mr. Dog must stay and have some, and by and by they made him promise to spend the day with them and be there when the Robin and Squirrel and Mr. Turtle and Jack Rabbit came, which he did.

And it was snowing hard outside, which made it a nicer Christmas than if it hadn't been, and when all the others came they brought presents, too. And when they saw Mr. Dog dressed up as Santa Claus and heard how he'd gone to sleep and been caught, they laughed and laughed. And it snowed so hard that they had to stay all night, and after dinner they sat around the fire and told stories. And they had to stay the next night, too, and all that Christmas week. And I wish that I could tell you all that happened that week, but I can't, because I haven't time. But it was the very nicest Christmas that ever was in the Hollow Tree, or in the Big Deep Woods anywhere.

Christmas Eve

TICK-TOCK," said the Nursery Clock,
"Please remember that little sock:
Nannie, mend the hole in the toe;
The goodies will tumble out, you know.
Tick-tock, tick-tock,"
Said the clickity-clackity Nursery Clock.
"Hush, hush," said Santa Claus,
As he peeped inside the bedroom doors;
"I am looking around for a little sock,
Do you know where it is, please, Mr. Clock?"
"Tick-tock, tick-tock,
It hangs over there," said the Nursery Clock.
"Tick-tock," said the Nursery Clock,
And pointed straight at the little sock,
Oh, yes he did, for don't you see,
A clock has hands like you and me.
"Tick-tock, tick-tock;
I am always right," said the Nursery Clock.

FLORENCE HOATSON

157

Jolly
Old St. Nicholas

Jolly Old Saint Nicholas

JOLLY old Saint Nicholas,
  Lean your ear this way!
Don't you tell a single soul
  What I'm going to say;
Christmas Eve is coming soon;
  Now you dear old man,
Whisper what you'll bring to me;
  Tell me if you can.

When the clock is striking twelve,
  When I'm fast asleep,
Down the chimney broad and black,
  With your pack you'll creep;

All the stockings you will find
  Hanging in a row;
Mine will be the shortest one,
  You'll be sure to know.

Johnny wants a pair of skates;
  Susy wants a sled;
Nellie wants a picture book;
  Yellow, blue and red;

Now I think I'll leave to you
  What to give the rest;
Choose for me, dear Santa Claus,
  You will know the best.

AUTHOR UNKNOWN
From an old song.

Giant Grummer's
Christmas

By WILLIAM DANA STREET

GIANT GRUMMER was a very bad giant. He never kept Christmas.

Sometimes on Christmas Day he would sit all day in his huge castle, eating pickles and drinking vinegar. Christmas was a very sour day for Giant Grummer. Just to think of so many people being happy gave him a headache.

He was a very bad giant!

Sometimes on Christmas Eve Giant Grummer and his retainers would go over to the neighboring village and sit on top of the chimneys so that Santa Claus could not go down them to give his presents to the boys and girls.

Sometimes he would even chase Santa Claus and his reindeer all over the roofs of the village and drive them far away.

The reindeer did not like Giant Grummer. His clothes smelt of limburger cheese and it made Donner and Blitzen sick. Then Santa Claus would have to stop and get each of them a cup of hot water with a little soda in it. When they felt better he would drive on again.

Giant Grummer lived in a huge castle all made of limburger cheese! Now limburger cheese smells the strongest of all the cheeses. No one in the village could come within a mile of the castle without being overcome.

But Giant Grummer loved limburger cheese! He loved it so much that he kept eating away great chunks of the castle towers and walls. He had to have workmen busy all the time making repairs. He was a very bad giant!

One Christmas, Giant Grummer was worse than he had ever been before. He said that he was going over to the village on Christmas Eve after Santa Claus had been there and reach his long arm down every chimney. He said he was going to grab all the stockings around the fireplaces with all of the presents in them! All of the dolls, all of the toys and all of the candy!

Then he was going to carry them over to his castle, spread them out on the floor, and stamp on them until they were all broken to pieces. Giant Grummer was a very bad giant.

The villagers were terribly worried when they heard this. Some said, "We will have to keep Christmas on Thanksgiving Day."

Others said, "No, the Fourth of July will be better."

But the children said, "Santa Claus comes only on December 25 and that is the only really truly Christmas Day."

That settled it, but what should they do?

Now there was a prince in the village and his name was Topsy Turvey! He was only a little boy, but he was not at all afraid of the giant, nor of his castle all made of limburger cheese. For Topsy had found out how he could go right into the castle and have a lot of fun there playing tricks on the giant.

He had found out that if he turned his nose around upside down and left it that way, everything smelt just the opposite from what it usually did. Cologne smelt like castor oil and limburger cheese smelt like cookies and gingerbread.

When Topsy heard that Giant Grummer was going to steal all of the children's Christmas presents, he went right to the telephone and called up Santa Claus.

They had a long talk together and made a wonderful plan. You shall hear how it all worked out.

Now Giant Grummer had never hung up his stocking at Christmas! Not even when he was a little boy! His mother had told him that she didn't believe in Santa Claus.

But the fact was that Santa Claus knew that the smell of Limburger Castle would make his reindeer deathly sick. So he never tried to go there.

First of all then, Giant Grummer received a very nice letter from Santa Claus. It said:

Dear Giant Grummer

Why don't you and your retainers hang up your stockings on Christmas Eve? I have some very nice presents which I would like to put into them; this would be much more fun than stealing the children's presents.

Your good friend,

Santa Claus

"Ho! Ho!" said Giant Grummer, when he received this nice letter from Santa Claus. "Ho! Ho! I'll fool old Santa Claus. I'll hang up my biggest stocking and I'll watch him fill it. Then I'll dump the presents all on the floor. And I'll still have time to go over to the village and snatch all of the children's presents." And he rubbed his hands and stamped his feet.

Giant Grummer was a very bad giant.

So on Christmas Eve all the giants came into the big living room of the castle to hang up their stockings in front of the fireplace.

Giant Grummer took a nail and hammer and hung up his stocking. What a big stocking it was! It was all made of red flannel. It was so big that Topsy could hide in it if he wanted to.

Then Duke Gorgonzola hung up his stocking. It was made out of two steamer rugs. Then Baron Roquefort hung up his stocking. It was made out of stair carpet. And then Lord Edam hung— No! He never wore any stockings. So he hung up his stocking cap.

Then they all went to bed and lay very still. They tried to stay awake and watch for Santa Claus. But the first thing you knew they fell fast asleep and never saw Santa Claus at all.

At midnight, Prince Topsy Turvy met Santa Claus on the lawn in front of the palace in the village. How fine Santa Claus looked in his red suit with his sleigh and his eight reindeer!

"But how shall we ever dare to drive to Limburger Castle?" asked Santa Claus.

"I'll show you," Topsy answered.

Then he turned Santa's nose upside down! And they both turned around the noses of all the eight reindeer!

When they were all ready, Topsy jumped into the sleigh with Santa Claus and they started for the castle of Giant Grummer.

Faster and faster they went! For now Limburger Castle smelt like cookies and gingerbread; and Donner and Blitzen and all the other reindeer were very fond of cookies and gingerbread.

On they went, right up onto the roof of the castle.

Down the chimney went Santa Claus!

Down the chimney went Topsy right after him.

Down the chimney went the eight reindeer!

They thought they were going to find cookies and gingerbread!

When Santa Claus saw the huge stockings, he drew a

long breath. But at once he began to try to fill them.

First he put into each stocking a real live automobile, not just a toy one.

Then he put in big tin horns, as big as a barrel!

And then a whole lot of candy and cookies and gingerbread!

Then last of all Santa Claus pulled out of his pack a great many round, red cheeses.

They were made of the very oldest and strongest-smelling limburger cheese. They were just awful! Topsy had to turn his nose around twice. Santa Claus had to turn his nose around twice. Donner and Blitzen and all of the other reindeer had to have their noses turned around twice.

Santa Claus put four of these big cheeses on top of each of the stockings. Then he and the eight reindeer went up the chimney and drove away to fill stockings in the village.

But Prince Topsy Turvey hid behind the big clock on the mantelpiece.

Soon it was morning. But even before daylight Giant Grummer and his retainers were trooping into the room to look at their stockings.

Topsy made his voice big, just like the giants': "Stop! Don't dare touch your stocking or it will bite you!"

Giant Grummer and his retainers looked at each other in amazement. "Where does that voice come from?" they wondered.

"Will you promise to be good all day?" cried Topsy. They looked around for the voice.

They very much wanted to look into their stockings, but they were afraid. Suppose the stocking really should bite them. They had had mosquitoes bite them. They had had dogs bite them. But they had never had a stocking bite them. It must be horrible!

"Will you promise to be good all day?" Topsy repeated.

They all promised.

"Then you may look into your stockings," said Topsy.

But as soon as Giant Grummer found the big cheeses, he did not look for anything else. He just sat down on the floor and began to eat them. They tasted nicer to him than any candy or even than chocolate ice cream!

He took one big bite and his smile was as big as a dinner plate. He took another big bite and his smile was as big as a platter. He took a third bite and the cheese was all gone!

He ate up two whole cheeses. But when he tried to eat

the third, he could not go on. He was just too full.

His eyes began to close.

Soon he was fast asleep.

Giant Grummer slept all through Christmas morning!

He slept all through Christmas afternoon! He slept all through Christmas evening! And that is the reason why Giant Grummer was good all day Christmas.

He was sound asleep all day long!

And the boys and girls in the village found their stockings full of Christmas gifts.

Unworthy

I HUNG up a stocking for Tippy, my pup,
To hold what old Santa might bring.
But that naughty puppy chewed holes in the sock!
He doesn't deserve anything!

INEZ GEORGE GRIDLEY

Jimmy Scarecrow's Christmas

By MARY E. WILKINS FREEMAN

JIMMY SCARECROW led a sad life in the winter. Jimmy's greatest grief was his lack of occupation. He liked to be useful, and in winter he was absolutely of no use at all.

He wondered how many such miserable winters he would have to endure. He was a young Scarecrow, and this was his first one. He was strongly made, and although his wooden joints creaked a little when the wind blew he did not grow in the least rickety. Every morning, when the wintry sun peered like a hard yellow eye across the dry corn-stubble, Jimmy felt sad, but at Christmas time his heart nearly broke.

On Christmas Eve Santa Claus came in his sledge heaped high with presents, urging his team of reindeer across the field. He was on his way to the farmhouse where Betsey lived with her Aunt Hannah.

Betsey was a very good little girl with very smooth yellow curls, and she had a great many presents. Santa Claus had a large wax doll-baby for her on his arm, tucked up against the fur collar of his coat. He was afraid to trust it in the pack, lest it get broken.

When poor Jimmy Scarecrow saw Santa Claus his heart gave a great leap. "Santa Claus! Here I am!" he cried out, but Santa Claus did not hear him.

"Santa Claus, please give me a little present. I was good all summer and kept the crows out of the corn," pleaded the poor Scarecrow in his choking voice, but Santa Claus passed by with a merry halloo and a great clamor of bells.

Then Jimmy Scarecrow stood in the corn-stubble and shook with sobs until his joints creaked. "I am of no use in the world, and everybody has forgotten me," he moaned. But he was mistaken.

The next morning Betsey sat at the window holding her Christmas doll-baby, and she looked out at Jimmy Scarecrow standing alone in the field amidst the corn-stubble.

"Aunt Hannah?" said she. Aunt Hannah was making a crazy patchwork quilt, and she frowned hard at a triangular piece of red silk and circular piece of pink, wondering how to fit them together. "Well?" said she.

"Did Santa Claus bring the Scarecrow any Christmas present?"

"No, of course he didn't."

"Why not?"

"Because he's a Scarecrow. Don't ask silly questions."

"I wouldn't like to be treated so, if I were a Scarecrow," said Betsey, but her Aunt Hannah did not hear her. She was busy cutting a triangular snip out of the round piece of pink silk so the piece of red silk could be feather-stitched into it.

It was snowing hard out of doors, and the north wind blew. The Scarecrow's poor old coat got whiter and whiter with snow. Sometimes he almost vanished in the thick white storm. Aunt Hannah worked until the middle of the afternoon on her crazy quilt. Then she got up and spread it out over the sofa with an air of pride.

"There," said she, "that's done, and that makes the eighth. I've got one for every bed in the house, and I've given four away. I'd give this away if I knew of anybody that wanted it."

Aunt Hannah put on her hood and shawl, and drew some blue yarn stockings on over her shoes, and set out through the snow to carry a slice of plum-pudding to her sister Susan, who lived down the road. Half an hour after Aunt Hannah had gone Betsey put her little red plaid shawl over her head, and ran across the field to Jimmy Scarecrow. She carried her new doll-baby smuggled up under her shawl.

"Wish you Merry Christmas!" she said to Jimmy Scarecrow.

"Wish you the same," said Jimmy, but his voice was choked with sobs, and was also muffled, for his old hat had slipped down to his chin. Betsey looked pitifully at the old hat fringed with icicles, like frozen tears, and the old snow-laden coat. "I've brought you a Christmas present," said she, and with that she tucked her doll-baby inside Jimmy Scarecrow's coat, sticking its tiny feet into a pocket.

"Thank you," said Jimmy Scarecrow faintly.

"You're welcome," said she. "Keep her under your overcoat, so the snow won't wet her and she won't catch cold; she's delicate."

"Yes, I will," said Jimmy Scarecrow, and he tried hard

to bring one of his stiff, outstretched arms around to clasp the doll-baby.

"Don't you feel cold in that old summer coat?" asked Betsey.

"If I had a little exercise, I should be warm," he replied. But he shivered, and the wind whistled through his rags.

"You wait a minute," said Betsey, and was off across the field.

Jimmy Scarecrow stood in the corn-stubble, with the doll-baby under his coat, and waited, and soon Betsey was back again with Aunt Hannah's crazy quilt trailing in the snow behind her.

"Here," said she, "here is something to keep you warm," and she folded the crazy quilt around the Scarecrow and pinned it.

"Aunt Hannah wants to give it away if anybody wants it," she explained. "She's got so many crazy quilts in the house now she doesn't know what to do with them. Good-bye—be sure you keep the doll-baby covered up." And with that she ran across the field, and left Jimmy Scarecrow alone with the crazy quilt and the doll-baby.

The bright flash of colours under Jimmy's hat-brim dazzled his eyes, and he felt a little alarmed. "I hope this quilt is harmless if it *is* crazy," he said. But the quilt was warm, and he dismissed his fears. Soon the doll-baby whimpered, but he creaked his joints a little, and that amused it, and he heard it cooing inside his coat.

Jimmy Scarecrow had never felt so happy in his life as he did for an hour or so. But after that the snow began to turn to rain, and the crazy quilt was soaked through and through: and not only that, but his coat and the poor doll-baby. It cried pitifully for a while, and then it was still, and he was afraid it was dead.

It grew very dark, and the rain fell in sheets, the snow melted, and Jimmy Scarecrow stood halfway up his old boots in water. He was saying to himself that the saddest hour of his life had come, when suddenly he again heard Santa Claus' sleigh-bells and his merry voice talking to his reindeer. It was after midnight, Christmas was over, and Santa was hastening home to the North Pole.

"Santa Claus! dear Santa Claus!" cried Jimmy Scarecrow with a great sob, and that time Santa Claus heard him and drew rein.

"Who's there?" he shouted out of the darkness.

"It's only me," replied the Scarecrow.

"Who me?" shouted Santa Claus.

"Jimmy Scarecrow!"

Santa got out of his sledge and waded up. "Have you been standing here ever since corn was ripe?" he asked pityingly, and Jimmy replied that he had.

"What's that over your shoulders?" Santa Claus continued, holding up his lantern.

"It's a crazy quilt."

"And what are you holding under your coat?"

"The doll-baby that Betsey gave me, and I'm afraid it's dead," poor Jimmy Scarecrow sobbed.

"Nonsense!" cried Santa Claus. "Let me see it!" And with that he pulled the doll-baby out from under the Scarecrow's coat, and patted its back, and shook it a little, and it began to cry, and then to crow. "It's all right," said Santa Claus. "This is the doll-baby I gave Betsey, and it is not at all delicate. It went through the measles, and the chicken-pox, and the mumps, and the whooping-cough, before it left the North Pole. Now get into the sledge, Jimmy Scarecrow, and bring the doll-baby and the crazy quilt. I have never had any quilts that weren't in their right minds at the North Pole, but maybe I can cure this one. Get in!" Santa chirruped to his reindeer, and they drew the sledge up close in a beautiful curve.

"Get in, Jimmy Scarecrow, and come with me to the North Pole!" he cried.

"Please, how long shall I stay?" asked Jimmy Scarecrow.

"Why, you are going to live with me," replied Santa Claus. "I've been looking for a person like you for a long time."

"Are there any crows to scare away at the North Pole? I want to be useful," Jimmy Scarecrow said, anxiously.

"No," answered Santa Claus, "but I don't want you to scare away crows. I want you to scare away Arctic Explorers. I can keep you in work for a thousand years, and scaring away Arctic Explorers from the North Pole is much more important than scaring away crows from corn. Why, if they found the Pole, there wouldn't be a piece an inch long left in a week's time, and the earth would cave in like an apple without a core! They would whittle it all to pieces, and carry it away in their pockets for souvenirs. Come along; I am in a hurry."

"I will go on two conditions," said Jimmy. "First I want to make a present to Aunt Hannah and Betsey, next Christmas."

"You shall make them any present you choose. What else?"

"I want some way provided to scare the crows out of the corn next summer, while I am away," said Jimmy.

"That is easily managed," said Santa Claus. "Just wait a minute."

Santa took his stylographic pen out of his pocket, went with his lantern close to one of the fence-posts, and wrote these words upon it:

NOTICE TO CROWS

Whichever crow shall hereafter hop, fly, or flop into this field during the absence of Jimmy Scarecrow, and therefrom purloin, steal, or abstract corn, shall be instantly, in a twinkling and a trice, turned snow-white, and be ever after a disgrace, a byword and a reproach to his whole race.

Per order of SANTA CLAUS.

"The corn will be safe now," said Santa Claus. "Get in." Jimmy got into the sledge and they flew away over the fields, out of sight, with merry halloos and a great clamour of bells.

The next morning there was much surprise at the farmhouse, when Aunt Hannah and Betsey looked out of the window and the Scarecrow was not in the field holding out his stiff arms over the corn stubble. Betsey had told Aunt Hannah she had given away the crazy quilt and the doll-baby, but had been scolded very little.

"You must not give away anything of yours again without asking permission," said Aunt Hannah. "And you have no right to give anything of mine, even if you know I don't want it. Now both my pretty quilt and your beautiful doll-baby are spoiled."

That was all Aunt Hannah had said. She thought she would send John after the quilt and the doll-baby next morning as soon as it was light.

But Jimmy Scarecrow was gone, and the crazy quilt and the doll-baby with him. John, the servant-man, searched everywhere, but not a trace of them could he find. "They must have all blown away, mum," he said to Aunt Hannah.

"We shall have to have another scarecrow next summer," said she.

But the next summer there was no need of a scarecrow, for not a crow came past the fence-post on which Santa Claus had written his notice to crows. The cornfield was never so beautiful, and not a single grain was stolen by a crow, and everybody wondered at it, for they could not read the crow-language in which Santa had written.

"It is a great mystery to me why the crows don't come into our cornfield, when there is no scarecrow," said Aunt Hannah.

But she had a still greater mystery to solve when Christmas came round again. Then she and Betsey had each a strange present. They found them in the sitting-room on Christmas morning. Aunt Hannah's present was her old crazy quilt, remodelled, with every piece cut square and true, and matched exactly to its neighbour.

"Why, it's my old crazy quilt, but it isn't crazy now!" cried Aunt Hannah, and her very spectacles seemed to glisten with amazement.

Betsey's present was her doll-baby of the Christmas before; but the doll was a year older. She had grown an inch, and could walk and say, "Mamma," and "How do?" She was changed a good deal, but Betsey knew her at once. "It's my doll-baby!" she cried, and snatched her up and kissed her.

But neither Aunt Hannah nor Betsey ever knew that the quilt and the doll were Jimmy Scarecrow's Christmas presents to them.

Santa Claus at the North Pole

By RICHARD EVELYN BYRD

IT WAS the night before Christmas. My plan for the first human flight across the North Pole was practically complete. To the world at large it was all a secret. Only a trusted few were in my confidence. Then without the slightest warning I found myself facing an unexpected crisis. Three people to whom I had told nothing suddenly and simultaneously confronted me with a terrific question. This question was delivered with the savage directness of a dagger thrust.

The three people were Katharine, Bolling, and Dickie Byrd, aged three, four and six, respectively.

The question was: "Daddy, will you see Santa Claus?"

It staggered me. Somehow they had learned their father was going to attempt an extraordinary thing. Then I played the coward. I said: "I will tell you in the morning."

"Promise?" from all three at once.

"I promise."

Three small white figures ducked up the stairs. There was giggling and skylarking. Then a chiding voice we all loved:

> " 'Twas the night before Christmas, and all through
>   the house
> Not a creature was stirring, not even a mouse . . ."

Out clicked a light. "I'm asleep!" shouted Junior.

"And I. And I," echoed the others.

Christmas morning dawned bright and clear and cold. We had the stockings in bed. There was a vast deal of thrills and chortling joy. But before the day was far along they all remembered their question. By now I was prepared. "No, I shan't see Santa Claus," I told Katharine and Bolling and Dickie. "But when I get back I'll tell you all about his place at the North Pole."

There, I had done it: I was committed. My fate was sealed when Dickie, the elder, in the presence of the others gave me a penetrating look and said:

"But there is a Santa Claus, Daddy, isn't there?"

"Of course there is a Santa Claus!" I fairly shouted.

In that moment was created the greatest problem of my

forthcoming polar flight. One who has not lied to a child could never understand. I had baldly and without reservation told my three babies something about which I myself was not sure. I had told them there was a Santa Claus. How did I know? I had never seen him. But perhaps in the course of this great adventure I should find that after all Santa Claus does exist.

It began to look that way when, after many disappointments, some fine generous friends gave me the money I needed for my voyage.

A splendid gentleman made it possible for me a few weeks later to get the ship I wanted.

"Won't he do?" I asked the mother of the three whom I had promised to satisfy. "He even looks like Santa Claus. I think I could get him to come around and talk to the babies."

But she spurned the plan. "He's just a man who helped you out, isn't he? He isn't Santa Claus." She came a step nearer. "Surely you believe there is a Santa Claus, don't you?" she said, a little fiercely, I thought.

I mopped my brow. It was April now and no weather for such talk. Also things weren't going as well as they might.

"I don't know whether there is a Santa Claus or not," I said lamely.

A few days later the little steamer *Chantier* with my plane and a crew of brave volunteers set sail. For two weeks she plowed her way northward toward the region of eternal ice and snow. She reached Spitzbergen safely, and we landed the plane through grinding floes.

Finally we hopped off for the Pole. Up into the blue sky our huge noisy bird winged her way. My good friend Floyd Bennett sat at the wheel. Calm and unafraid he held our course northward while I consulted the instruments of flight on which our lives depended.

Behind us dropped the narrow, berg-dotted harbor in which lay the ship. To our right, slipping swiftly by, were mountain peaks dazzling white in their cloaks of snow. Presently they, too, were gone. We emerged into a strange world, a world of blue sky above and white ice below.

There was nothing else. Not a living thing: no birds in the air, no bears on the ice. Not a strip of land since Spitzbergen had sunk beneath the southern horizon. Not even a rock. A dead, dead world.

This, then, was the realm of Santa Claus. In the yearly Christmastide this ice field beneath us would be shrouded in the darkness of the six months' Arctic night. Perhaps the flaming aurora might cast its fitful rays across the heavens for a few hours, or the milky beams of a pale midwinter moon cast blue-black shadows behind each upended floe. A million bright stars would sparkle in space. But the vast ice fields would remain empty and unmoving. In the sunless nights of the North the Christmas hours would silently file by.

A flash of all this came to me as I glanced through the window of my plane hurtling its way through space. How strange it seemed that a huge, black, useless, bitterly cold portion of the earth's surface should once a year become so important! And it *is* important when it bears upon the lives of boys and girls all over the world who believe there is a Santa Claus.

"But is there a Santa Claus?"

I have wondered since what Floyd Bennett, my pilot, would have thought if I had written that question on our communication pad and handed it to him in the midst of our flight.

Then came the great moment. We were at the North Pole. Below us was nothing but ice. Ice spread to a clear horizon all around. Aged bergs huddled among the floes. Pressure ridges drifted deep with snow zigzagged across the white pack. Ugly scars over big floes showed where the tide had torn them apart, later to be healed by the bitter cold.

So this was the home of Santa Claus. This was the apex of the globe whence he sped southward each Christmas Eve to fill millions of stockings. This bleak icicled wilderness was the site of his renowned workshop. This was where he kept the record book of good deeds and bad against the names of little folk throughout the world. This was the fount of Christmas happiness from which flowed the sweetest wine of all the ages.

At least, so it was said. But was it true? Was there a Santa Claus?

I began to doubt it almost in the same breath. For trouble came. One engine looked as if it were going to die from an oil leak. Later my sextant, by which we were to navigate home, fell from the chart board and was broken. The other two engines might keep us up at a pinch. But if they did we might be lost owing to our inability to fix our position.

Brave Floyd Bennett shook his head. His optimism was dented by these two catastrophes. The fact we were prepared to march back over the ice did not help much. That was a desperate chance which we hoped we wouldn't be forced to take.

We swung about and set our compass course for home. But we could not tell if we were being forced adrift by the wind. We could not be sure at what moment the leaking oil would cause us to drop upon the wild and ragged ice below.

Yet we were too near the breaking point to feel real fear. For thirty-six hours before the hop-off we had not slept. We had now been in the air for many more hours. Nervous strain of the flight had told heavily on our strength.

In a sort of fitful petulance I thought back again to the comfort and safety of home. A curious flash of anger swept over me when the picture of my children came into my mind. I meant so much to their future. And here I was dangling on the brink of death.

I glanced at Bennett. His face told the story of his forebodings. He threw a look at the wrecked sextant and shook his head. I read his thought: Could we find our way without navigating? It was a gamble, all right.

I set my teeth. How could there be any Santa Claus in a world so cruel? The little faith I had had was slipping away. I could almost see the future. We should slither down on the jagged ice floes. We could not help wrecking the plane. We should crawl out and start the long trek home.

Greenland, far west, was our only hope of escape. For months we should stagger onward through the snow and the bitter winds. We should die by inches.

What could my Lady tell the youngsters? Their Daddy had gone to the land of Santa Claus. He had never returned. The very thought made me shudder.

Time passed. We ought to sight land by now. But there was no land. I was right; Bennett was right. We had failed even though we had reached the Pole.

Suddenly my straining eyes caught a shadow on the horizon. A low curving cloudlike form stood there in the south. It couldn't be a cloud. Then I knew: It was land! We were saved! I should get back home. Little else mattered. What should I tell them? What would any man tell them after skimming so close to the end as had I?

"There is a Santa Claus! I know it, for I've been to the Pole and seen!"

Is There a Santa Claus?

W E TAKE PLEASURE IN answering at once and thus prominently the communication below, expressing at the same time our great gratification that its faithful author is numbered among the friends of THE SUN:

"DEAR EDITOR—I am 8 years old.

"Some of my little friends say there is no SANTA CLAUS.

"Papa says 'If you see it in THE SUN it's so.'

"Please tell me the truth, is there a SANTA CLAUS?

"VIRGINIA O'HANLON

"115 West Ninety-fifth street."

From an editorial by FRANCIS P. CHURCH *in* THE SUN (*New York*), *September 21st, 1897.*

VIRGINIA, your little friends are wrong. They have been affected by the skepticism of a skeptical age. They do not believe except they see. They think that nothing can be which is not comprehensible by their little minds. All minds, VIRGINIA, whether they be men's or children's are little. In this great universe of ours man is a mere insect, an ant, in his intellect, as compared with the boundless world about him, as measured by the intelligence capable of grasping the whole of truth and knowledge.

Yes, VIRGINIA, there is a SANTA CLAUS. He exists as certainly as love and generosity and devotion exist, and you know that they abound and give to your life its highest beauty and joy. Alas! how dreary would be the world if there were no SANTA CLAUS! It would be as dreary as if there were no Virginias. There would be no childlike faith then, no poetry, no romance to make tolerable this existence. We should have no enjoyment, except in sense and sight. The eternal light with which childhood fills the world would be extinguished.

Not believe in SANTA CLAUS! You might as well not believe in fairies! You might get your papa to hire men to watch in all the chimneys on Christmas Eve to catch SANTA CLAUS, but even if they did not see SANTA CLAUS coming down, what would that prove? Nobody sees SANTA CLAUS, but that is no sign that there is no SANTA CLAUS. The most real things in the world are those that neither children nor men can see. Did you ever see fairies dancing on the lawn? Of course not, but that's no proof that they are not there. Nobody can conceive or imagine all the wonders there are unseen and unseeable in the world.

You tear apart the baby's rattle and see what makes the noise inside, but there is a veil covering the unseen world which not the strongest man, nor even the united strength of all the strongest men that ever lived, could tear apart. Only faith, fancy, poetry, love, romance, can push aside that curtain and view and picture the supernal beauty and glory beyond. Is it all real? Ah, VIRGINIA, in all this world there is nothing else real and abiding.

No SANTA CLAUS! Thank God! he lives, and he lives forever. A thousand years from now, VIRGINIA, nay, ten times ten thousand years from now, he will continue to make glad the heart of childhood.

Piccola

Piccola

POOR sweet Piccola! Did you hear
What happened to Piccola, children dear?
'Tis seldom fortune such favor grants
As fell to this little maid of France.

'Twas Christmas time, and her parents poor
Could hardly drive the wolf from the door,
Striving with poverty's patient pain,
Only to live until summer again.

No gifts for Piccola! Sad were they
When dawned the morning of Christmas day;
Their little darling no joy might stir,
Saint Nicholas nothing would bring to her.

But Piccola did not doubt at all
That something beautiful must befall
Every child upon Christmas day;
And so she slept till the dawn was gray.

And full of faith when at last she woke,
She stole to her shoes as the morning broke;
Such sounds of gladness filled the air
'Twas plain Saint Nicholas had been there.

In rushed Piccola sweet, half wild;
Never was seen such a joyful child.
"See what the good saint brought!" she cried
And mother and father must peep inside.

Now such a story who ever heard?
There was only a little shivering bird.
A sparrow that in at the window flew
Had crept into Piccola's wooden shoe!

"How good poor Piccola must have been!"
She cried, as happy as any queen;
While the starving sparrow she fed and warmed
She danced with rapture, she was so charmed.

Children, this story I tell to you
Of Piccola sweet and her bird is true;
In the far-off land of France they say
Still do they live to this very day.

CELIA THAXTER

Mikulás, Bearer of Gifts

I
T HAD BEEN snowing since last night. The first light flakes fell just before bedtime, drifting into the yellow shaft of light, shining through the kitchen window. Kate and Jancsi ran out trying to catch some of them. It wasn't very cold then, and the flakes melted as soon as they fell on the ground. By morning the drifting flakes had changed into a real snowstorm. Deep drifts had piled up against the walls, and the barns and stables were just gray shadows behind the veil of swirling snow. An icy wind howled around the house.

Inside, the house was warm and bright with candlelight.

This story is from the book THE GOOD MASTER *by* KATE SEREDY.

There were huge bowls full of chopped meat and spices on the table. Mother was making sausages. The pig had been killed the day before. Father made a roaring fire in the smokehouse, and hams and shoulders were hung up in the chimney. Kate was busy filling sausages and tying up the ends with cord.

"You know what day it is?" she asked Jancsi with shining eyes. "It's the sixth of December! Mikulá Day! Tonight we'll put our boots on the windowsill and Mikulás will fill them with gifts and candy."

"Did you ever see him?" whispered Jancsi.

Kate shook her head. "I tried often, but I always fell asleep before he came. My father said Mikulás wears a long red coat edged with white fur, a red hat, black shiny boots, and he carries a bag of gifts." She paused for a second, then turned to Jancsi confidentially. "Do you think he is real or only make-believe?"

"I don't know. Let's try to stay awake tonight; maybe we'll catch him," said Jancsi.

Father overheard the conversation. He smiled. "You won't have to catch him. We will go to town and bring him home with us—he wrote me that he would come on the train this time."

"Oh, Father!" Jancsi was delighted. "We'll take the sleigh, won't we?"

"We'll have to. It's snowing harder every minute. Look, it's almost dark now and it can't be more than two o'clock."

Kate's eyes were sparkling. "A sleigh ride—oh, good! I've never been on a sleigh ride. But Uncle Márton, is Mikulás really coming? I mean, a *real* Mikulás, red coat and bag of gifts and everything?"

Father nodded. "With a big bag of gifts, the best Mikulás anybody could wish for. He's making a special trip for you and Jancsi because you have been such very, very good little farm hands."

Jancsi and Kate were puzzled. They strongly suspected that the red-coated Mikulás, the mysterious bearer of gifts, wasn't real. Nobody had ever met him. He came and went in the night, leaving gifts and happiness behind. Jancsi thought perhaps it was Father who always filled his boots, but now he had said they would actually bring him home from the train! It was all very mysterious.

"When do we start?" he asked.

"Around four o'clock. Pista will do the chores tonight. It's a holiday for you and Kate. We'll put bells on the sleigh and you two put on your Sunday clothes. And, Mother—you will make a good holiday supper for us, won't you?"

"Sausages! Does Mikulás eat regular food? Does he like sausages?" asked Kate.

"He used to love them the last time I saw him!" Father laughed.

"When did you see him, Father?"

"Just twenty years ago," said Father.

Later on Jancsi and Father went out to get the sleigh ready. The snow was so deep they had to shovel a path to the stables. The world was wrapped in snow, even their voices sounding muffled and distant.

Kate was so excited, she had to ask Mother to help her button up her dress. It was a new dress, even prettier than the one Mother had made her for Easter. This one had a blue woolen shirred skirt with white and red flowers embroidered around the hem. A tight little blue jacket edged with lamb's fur went with it. The jacket had red buttons all the way down the front. Kate, with her little fur cap and red boots, looked as pretty as a picture. Jancsi had a new winter suit, too. It was exactly like Father's suit—blue wool, the coat lined with fur, and even the brass buttons on it the same as Father's.

When Father came in to carry out the sheepskins, he

smiled at Kate. "I think your—er—I think Mikulás will have a great surprise tonight. Look at our 'delicate' Kate, Mother! Isn't she the picture of health? He'll never know her!"

"He never saw me before, Uncle Márton. I was always in bed when he came."

Mother laughed and shook her head. "Father, Father. You'll spoil the surprise if you don't watch out. Here's your hat now. One—two—three—out with you or you will be late for the train."

She came out to tuck the covers around them. It was bitterly cold. When Kate looked around as the sleigh turned onto the road, all she could see was the bright square of the kitchen window. Everything else—house, barns, stables —was blotted out. Soon the sleigh was traveling in a dark no-man's land. The sleigh bells were cheerful; without them there would have been utter silence. The lanterns were comforting; without them there would have been utter darkness.

"One more day like this and we will be snowed in," said Father. Nobody answered. Kate and Jancsi were snuggled deep under the sheepskins.

Only the dim lights of many small windows told

them that they were driving through the village. The street was silent and deserted. Even the town was a very quiet place tonight. Father left Jancsi and Kate in the sleigh and went into the station to see if Mikulás had arrived.

"Oh, Jancsi. I'm so excited I can hardly sit still," whispered Kate. "Do you think he is really coming?"

"Father said he was coming—so he *is* coming!" said Jancsi stoutly. But he watched the door just as anxiously as Kate. They heard the train come in—stop—then puff and groan again and go. People came out, got into the few waiting sleighs and coaches, and drove away. Then the street was empty again, with only the wind howling around the dark buildings.

"Here they come," cried Kate. Father and Mikulás walked toward the sleigh. They were carrying big bags over their shoulders.

"Mikulás," whispered Jancsi, peering eagerly at the mysterious figure. "He *must* be the real Mikulás—red coat, red cap, black boots, just like his pictures!"

Kate nodded. "And look, he has long white hair and a white beard. He looks very old."

Father lifted the bags into the sleigh. Then he turned to

Mikulás. "Now my dear—Mikulás—you had a long, cold trip. We'll just let Jancsi do the driving. You and I will sit in the back and talk about old times."

Mikulás looked at Kate intently, but he did not say anything. He climbed in next to Father, and Jancsi started the horses. Jancsi was more puzzled than ever. His father was talking to the mysterious Mikulás as if he were talking to a regular everyday man. Kate wiggled on the seat—she kept turning around trying to see the face of Mikulás. But it was very dark. Besides, if she stretched her neck too far out of her sheepskin, the wind stuck a very unpleasant icy finger down her back.

When they reached the village, Father leaned forward. "Stop at the church square, Jancsi. Mikulás has gifts for the village children. He will leave something at every house."

The houses were dark. Village people go to bed early in the winter. Father gave Jancsi and Kate lanterns to carry. He and Mikulás took the big bags and they walked to the nearest house. Then for the first time Mikulás spoke. His voice was strangely muffled. "Hold up the lantern, Kate, let me see my list."

He produced a long sheet of paper. "Hm! Two children in this house, good children, too. What do you think they would like, Jancsi? Open the big bag, let's see what we have."

The bag revealed an astonishing assortment of gifts. Toy animals, dolls, pocketknives, bags of candy, warm stockings, mittens, boxes of crayons, books, small tools, games—everything to make children happy.

Jancsi was thinking hard. He knew every child in the village. These two were girls—one of them three years old, the other six. "Dolls—I think they would like dolls best—or perhaps some candy."

They found the little shoes on the windowsill. Kate put a small doll near each shoe *and* a little bag of candy. Slowly they walked from house to house.

"Isn't this just wonderful, Jancsi?" whispered Kate. "It makes me feel all warm and good inside."

"Me, too. It's better than the fair."

They came to the very last house. There were two worn little shoes on the windowsill, but the big bags were empty. Mikulás looked at Kate. "I haven't anything more, only the gifts I brought for you and Jancsi. We'll have to go home," he said in his strange muffled voice.

"Oh, oh, no, please!" cried Kate. "I would rather leave my gifts here, wouldn't you, Jancsi?"

"I would! Please, Mikulás, won't you let us give our things to these children? We—we had a wonderful time anyway, just going around with you."

Mikulás didn't say a word. He brought a small package from the sleigh. There were two pairs of warm mittens in the package, two big picture books, two boxes of candy, and, best of all, two beautiful riding whips. He handed them to Jancsi. Jancsi looked at them longingly for a second. He looked at Kate. But he shook his head. He remembered the two boys in this last house. Their father was the poorest man in the village. Then he smiled at Mikulás. "These are beautiful gifts, but these are very poor children. Thank you for letting us leave them here."

Mikulás made a queer noise in his throat. It was something between a laugh and a sob. When he spoke, his voice was huskier than ever. "Thank you, Jancsi, and thank you, Kate. You have made me very happy tonight."

Kate squeezed Jancsi's hand. On the way back to the sleigh she whispered to him: "I have heard his voice before —only I can't remember where. You know, Jancsi, I just *can't* believe that he is the fairy-story Mikulás. He sounds too real!"

"I think so, too," said Jancsi. "But tonight feels like a fairy story just the same. Father looks like he always does when he has a big surprise for us. Anything might happen!"

Wisps of conversations came from the back of the sleigh: "Gypsies—round up—sausages—Milky." Father was telling Mikulás about Kate and Jancsi. A hearty laugh made Kate turn around quickly, and just as quickly it changed into a hoarse cough. Where had she heard that laugh before?

Mother must have heard the sleigh bells because she was standing in the open door as they reached the gate. Pista was waiting for them. "I'll take care of everything, Mister Nagy. You just stay with the family tonight."

The table was set beautifully; it was a blaze of candle-light and color. There was a roaring fire in the big stove. Mother wore her best Sunday clothes, too. She came forward now, smiling happily. "Welcome home, Mikulás," she cried. And to the astonishment of Kate and Jancsi gave him a good hug and kiss. "Here, sit by the fire and get warm. I'll have supper on the table in a minute."

"Thank you, my dear. It does feel like coming home at last," said Mikulás.

"Daddy!" screamed Kate, running toward him. "You are —you *are* my daddy! Take off your hat, please. And those white whiskers. Now I know where I had heard your voice before. Oh, Daddy!"

The rest was mumbled against the shoulder of Mikulás,

who held Kate very close to him, while Mother, half laughing, half crying, tried to peel off his false white hair and beard.

When he finally discarded all his Mikulás disguise, Kate's father looked startlingly like his brother. He had the same strong, kind face, the same honest, merry eyes. He held out his hand to Jancsi. "Come here, Son, let me take a good look at you."

Jancsi advanced cautiously. He liked his uncle very much at first sight, but perhaps he would want to kiss him, or something—men didn't kiss each other! But no—Uncle Sándor shook hands with him gravely and did not attempt to make a baby of Jancsi.

"I am very glad you came, Uncle Sándor. It's much nicer to have you than to have Mikulás." Then he smiled at Father. "I knew you had a secret, Father, you had your surprise face on—kind of twinkling and shining all over."

Uncle Sándor laughed. "I had the hardest time trying to change my voice, and those whiskers were a punishment. They tickled my nose so."

"We didn't know what to think, did we, Kate? But honestly, Father, is there a *real* Mikulás?" asked Jancsi.

"You know who the real Mikulás is? He is a different person to every child. He is always the one who loves you best in the world. We left beautiful gifts for the village children, but each of them will find some other gift, too, tomorrow morning. Perhaps it will be a very, very simple little gift, but it will be precious to those children because it was given with the greatest love."

"But who is he, really?" persisted Jancsi. "Just somebody in a fairy story?"

"No, Jancsi," said Kate's father. "I'll tell you who the real Mikulás was. His name was really Nicholas. He was a bishop in Russia about fifteen hundred years ago. While he was alive he used to go around doing good, helping people—he always had a gift for children. He did so much good in his life that after he died people called him Saint Nicholas. Then they made him patron saint of Russia and the patron saint of all children. His day, which is the sixth of December, became a holiday in Russia. They celebrated his day by giving each other, and especially the children, whom Saint Nicholas loved so much, beautiful gifts in his name. This habit spread all over the world. In some countries he comes on Christmas Day. To us he comes today. We believe that on Christmas Eve the Christ Child walks on earth and leaves gifts for everybody."

Kate looked up. "He does, really, doesn't he, Daddy?"

Kate's father smiled. "He does really, Kate, my dear. He comes, and puts love and tenderness in our hearts, so much love for each other that it overflows and turns into gifts we find under the Christmas tree."

"I think it is beautiful—the way you tell it, Daddy. Now I understand it. It isn't just secrets and make-believe like sometimes I thought it was."

The Festival of
Saint Nicholas

WE ALL KNOW HOW, before the Christmas tree began to flourish in the home life of our country, a certain "right jolly old elf," with "eight tiny reindeer," used to drive his sleigh-load of toys up to our housetops, and then bound down the chimney to fill the stockings so hopefully hung by the fireplace. His friends called him Santa Claus; and those who were most intimate ventured to say, "Old Nick." It was said that he originally came from Holland. Doubtless he did; but, if so, he certainly, like many other foreigners, changed his ways very much after landing upon our shores. In Holland, Saint Nicholas is a veritable saint,

This story is from the book HANS BRINKER, OR THE SILVER SKATES *by* MARY MAPES DODGE.

and often appears in full costume, with his embroidered robes glittering with gems and gold, his mitre, his crosier, and his jewelled gloves. *Here* Santa Claus comes rollicking along on the 25th of December, our holy Christmas morn; but in Holland, Saint Nicholas visits earth on the 5th, a time especially appropriated to him. Early on the morning of the 6th, he distributes his candies, toys, and treasures, and then vanishes for a year.

Christmas Day is devoted by the Hollanders to church-rites and pleasant family visiting. It is on Saint Nicholas Eve that their young people become half wild with joy and expectation. To some of them it is a sorry time; for the saint is very candid, and, if any of them have been bad during the past year, he is quite sure to tell them so. Sometimes he carries a birch-rod under his arm, and advises the parents to give them scoldings in place of confections, and floggings instead of toys.

It was well that the boys hastened to their abodes on that bright winter evening; for, in less than an hour afterwards, the saint made his appearance in half the homes of Holland. He visited the king's palace, and in the selfsame moment appeared in Annie Bouman's comfortable home. Probably one of our silver half-dollars would have purchased all that his saintship left at the peasant Bouman's. But a half-dollar's worth will sometimes do for the poor what hundreds of dollars may fail to do for the rich: it makes them happy and grateful, fills them with new peace and love.

Hilda van Gleck's little brothers and sisters were in a high state of excitement that night. They had been admitted into the grand parlor: they were dressed in their best, and had been given two cakes apiece at supper. Hilda was as joyous as any. Why not? Saint Nicholas would never cross a girl of fourteen from his list, just because she was tall and looked almost like a woman. On the contrary, he would probably exert himself to do honor to such an august-looking damsel. Who could tell? So she sported and laughed and danced as gayly as the youngest, and was the soul of all their merry games. Father, mother, and grandmother looked on approvingly; so did grandfather, before he spread his large red handkerchief over his face, leaving only the top of his skullcap visible. This kerchief was his ensign of sleep.

Earlier in the evening, all had joined in the fun. In the general hilarity, there had seemed to be a difference only in bulk between grandfather and the baby. Indeed, a shade of solemn expectation, now and then flitting across the faces of the younger members, had made them seem rather more thoughtful than their elders.

Now the spirit of fun reigned supreme. The very flames danced and capered in the polished grate. A pair of prim candles, that had been staring at the astral lamp, began to wink at other candles far away in the mirrors. There was a long bell-rope suspended from the ceiling in the corner, made of glass beads, netted over a cord nearly as thick as your wrist. It generally hung in the shadow, and made no sign; but tonight it twinkled from end to end. Its handle of crimson glass sent reckless dashes of red at the papered wall, turning its dainty blue stripes into purple. Passers-by halted to catch the merry laughter floating through curtain and sash into the street, then skipped on their way with the startled consciousness that the village was wide awake. At last matters grew so uproarious that the grandsire's red kerchief came down from his face with a jerk. What decent old gentleman could sleep in such a racket! Mynheer van Gleck regarded his children with astonishment. The baby even showed symptoms of hysterics. It was high time to attend to business. Madame suggested that, if they wished to see the good Saint Nicholas, they should sing the same loving invitation that had brought him the year before.

The baby stared, and thrust his fist into his mouth, as Mynheer put him down upon the floor. Soon he sat erect, and looked with a sweet scowl at the company. With his lace and embroideries, and his crown of blue ribbon and whalebone (for he was not quite past the tumbling age), he looked like the king of the babies.

The other children, each holding a pretty willow basket, formed at once in a ring, and moved slowly around the little fellow, lifting their eyes meanwhile; for the saint to whom they were about to address themselves was yet in mysterious quarters.

Madame commenced playing softly upon the piano; soon the voices rose—gentle, youthful voices, rendered all the sweeter for their tremor—

"Welcome, friend! Saint Nicholas, welcome!
    Bring no rod for us tonight!
While our voices bid thee welcome,
    Every heart with joy is light.

"Tell us every fault and failing;
    We will bear thy keenest railing
    So we sing, so we sing:
    Thou shalt tell us everything!

Welcome, friend! Saint Nicholas, welcome!
Welcome to this merry band!
Happy children greet thee, welcome!
Thou are gladdening all the land.

"Fill each empty hand and basket;
'Tis thy little ones who ask it.
So we sing, so we sing:
Thou wilt bring us everything!"

During the chorus, sundry glances, half in eagerness, half in dread, had been cast towards the polished folding-doors. Now a loud knocking was heard. The circle was broken in an instant. Some of the little ones, with a strange mixture of fear and delight, pressed against their mother's knee. Grandfather bent forward, with his chin resting upon his hand; grandmother lifted her spectacles; Mynheer van Gleck, seated by the fireplace, slowly drew his meerschaum from his mouth; while Hilda and the other children settled themselves beside him in an expectant group.

The knocking was heard again.

"Come in," said Madame, softly.

The door slowly opened; and Saint Nicholas, in full array, stood before them. You could have heard a pin drop.

Soon he spoke. What a mysterious majesty in his voice! What kindliness in his tones!

"Karel van Gleck, I am pleased to greet thee, and thy honored *vrouw*, Kathrine, and thy son, and his good *vrouw*, Annie.

"Children, I greet ye all—Hendrick, Hilda, Broom, Katy, Huygens, and Lucretia. And thy cousins—Wolfert, Diedrich, Mayken, Voost, and Katrina. Good children ye have been, in the main, since I last accosted ye. Diedrich was rude at the Haarlem fair last fall; but he has tried to atone for it since. Mayken has failed, of late, in her lessons; and too many sweets and trifles have gone to her lips, and too few stivers to her charity-box. Diedrich, I trust, will be a polite, manly boy for the future; and Mayken will endeavor to shine as a student. Let her remember, too, that economy and thrift are needed in the foundation of a worthy and generous life. Little Katy has been cruel to the cat more than once. Saint Nicholas can hear the cat cry when its tail is pulled. I will forgive her, if she will remember from this hour that the smallest dumb creatures have feeling, and must not be abused."

As Katy burst into a frightened cry, the saint graciously remained silent until she was soothed.

"Master Broom," he resumed, "I warn thee that boys

who are in the habit of putting snuff upon the foot-stove of the school-mistress may one day be discovered, and receive a flogging—"

(Master Broom colored, and stared in great astonishment.)

"But, thou art such an excellent scholar, I shall make thee no further reproof.

"Thou, Hendrick, didst distinguish thyself in the archery match last Spring, and hit the bulls-eye, though the bird was swung before it to unsteady thine eye. I give thee credit for excelling in manly sport and exercise—though I must not unduly countenance thy boat-racing since it leaves thee too little time for thy proper studies.

"Lucretia and Hilda shall have a blessed sleep tonight. The consciousness of kindness to the poor, devotion in their souls, and cheerful, hearty obedience to household rule will render them happy

"With one and all I avow myself well content. Goodness, industry, benevolence and thrift have prevailed in your midst. Therefore, my blessing upon you—and may the New Year find all treading the paths of obedience, wisdom and love. Tomorrow you shall find more substantial proofs that I have been in your midst. Farewell!"

With these words came a great shower of sugar-plums, upon a linen sheet spread out in front of the doors. A general scramble followed. The children fairly tumbled over each other in their eagerness to fill their baskets. Madame cautiously held the baby down in their midst, till the chubby little fists were filled. Then the bravest of the youngsters sprang up and burst open the closed doors—in vain they peered into the mysterious apartment—Saint Nicholas was nowhere to be seen.

Soon there was a general rush to another room, where stood a table, covered with the finest and whitest of linen damask. Each child, in a flutter of excitement, laid a shoe upon it. The door was then carefully locked, and its key hidden in the mother's bedroom. Next followed good-night kisses, a grand family-procession to the upper floor, merry farewells at bedroom doors—and silence, at last, reigned in the Van Gleck mansion.

Early the next morning the door was solemnly unlocked and opened in the presence of the assembled household, when lo! a sight appeared proving Saint Nicholas to be a saint of his word!

Every shoe was filled to overflowing, and beside each stood many a colored pile. The table was heavy with its load of presents—candies, toys, trinkets, books and other articles. Every one had gifts, from grandfather down to the baby.

Little Katy clapped her hands with glee, and vowed, inwardly, that the cat should never know another moment's grief.

Hendrick capered about the room, flourishing a superb bow and arrows over his head. Hilda laughed with delight as she opened a crimson box and drew forth its glittering contents. The rest chuckled and said "Oh!" and "Ah!" over their treasures, very much as we did here in America on last Christmas day.

The Yule Elf's
Christmas Gift

By NORA BURGLON

I T WAS the day before Christmas. That, as everyone knew, was called Dipping Day in Sweden. It had been a fast day in the years gone by. People had dipped their bread into the broth kettle for supper that evening, and had not troubled sitting down to the table properly. However, the world had now become so topsy-turvy that it was only the wealthy who longer had any broth for the dipping.

When Christmas came it was the Yule Nisse who brought the gifts to the children of Norway and Sweden. He was supposed to be related to the little fellow that lived somewhere on their croft, and did little else all year long but bring good luck to the place.

At the moment Nicolina and her brother Sture were sitting on their doorstep, staring off across the snow-covered fields and thinking. Nor was it such flighty thinking as might have been done on any other day. They were alone, for their mother was staying to comfort the Widow Anderson.

Nicolina had just said that she thought it was no more than right that they should think of making a gift for the Christmas elf. After all, no one ever thought of giving him anything, in return for his kindness, she pointed out.

Her brother nodded gravely. So now here they were on Dipping Day, trying to plan some present for the Yule Nisse this Christmas. "There are the birch-twig porridge beaters which we made," said Sture.

"What would the Yule elf do with a porridge beater?" asked Nicolina. "But there are the mittens that I knit. We could give him a pair of mittens for Christmas."

"But those mittens are not his size," Sture complained.

No, that was right too. Had they not been made for Wood-cutter Ole Anderson, whose hands had been so big that they could match the paws of the largest bear in the zoo!

"The thing to do," said Sture, "is to take them to the market and trade them off for a pair that will fit the Yule elf."

Nicolina agreed, so they got upon their skis and hurried off into the dusk. Although the moon was rising off over the eastern hills, it was really little more than the middle of the afternoon. That was the way of things in Sweden, where in the summer there was nothing but daylight, and in the winter little else but darkness from December until March.

The two children hastened off eagerly for the market, but when they reached there it was to find that the mitten merchant had sold his last pair of "vantar," and had gone home. The children took their mittens from one merchant to another and asked if there was not something they might have in exchange. However, when the merchants heard that those mittens had been made for Big Ole, they shook their heads. That one had known nothing but bad luck from the time he was born until he broke through the ice of Wild Man's Beck and didn't manage to flounder out again. No, they wanted nothing of his, said they.

At length Nicolina and Sture had to strike off for home again, but it no longer felt like Dipping Day, there was such a big and heavy burden in their hearts. They had bought Big Ole's mitten wool with money they had earned picking mushrooms in the fall. It was sad enough to have lost their friend a few days before Christmas, without having people think bad-luck thoughts about his mittens.

As they passed the post office the Postmaster came out and called to them. "A letter has just arrived from America for the Colonel," said he, "and my rheumatism is so bad I can scarcely stir out the door. Could I get you to deliver it for me?" He came over to them in the snow, adding, "You know it would not be much of a Christmas for the Colonel without that letter."

Nicolina and Sture brightened a bit when they heard this. There was nothing like sharing the burden of somebody else, to lessen one's own. Well enough they knew about that letter from America. Although it never bore a return address, people said that it was from the Colonel's son, who had run away to sea twenty years before.

Now that Sture had that important American letter in his vest pocket, their own worry seemed half solved. With new cheerfulness the two sped toward the Colonel's house, skiing so swiftly that they scarcely noticed the Yule candles already lit in windows along the way. Now and then a sleigh passed them, with a glorious jingling of bells, and trailing behind the pitchy smell of the burning torches that flared from the dash.

Once the children glanced back, half in envy and half in wonder, at the horses, for they looked more like spirit than real. They were covered with nets that had sea shells sewed into them. Now with the frost glittering on the shells and the net, they seemed as part of the glimmer and solemnity of the stars.

The lights in the windows were already lit at the Colonel's house up the hill. There were seven candles in every window. No doubt they had been lit to welcome home the son that never came.

Nicolina and Sture now stood upon the wide and splendid porch, waiting for someone to come to the door and relieve them of their responsibility. It was one of the kitchen maids that came to answer the door, and she wore her Dipping Day apron still. When she heard that the two were bringing the Christmas letter from America she said, "Come in. I am sure the Colonel himself will want to speak to you."

So the two unfastened their skis and followed after the girl into the great room where the master of the manor lay. A Christmas tree stood near his bed, and under it were many parcels, tied with ribbons that shone like pure gold. It seemed that the Yule Nisse must already have made his visit here, and small wonder! It had no doubt required a whole day for him to get all those gifts delivered. The maids had said that there were always gifts under that tree for the son who had not returned. A wonder that the Yule elf did not know that the boy no longer lived there.

The Colonel's hands trembled as he took the letter from Sture. "Thank you. Thank you very much," said he, when they had explained about the Postmaster's rheumatism. He

then motioned the maid to his beside and whispered something to her.

The children glanced back at the Colonel, but he had
opened the letter and was reading it with avid eyes. He had
already forgotten about them.

The maid brought the two out into the dining hall where
a table stood, laden with food. It would stand so, set and
ready to serve anyone who came, during all the twenty days
of Christmas. Commencing with Saint Stephen's Day, which
was the day after Christmas, Yule-bucking parties would be
stopping at the house. Of course all who came must have
something to eat. It was considered bad luck for anyone to
come calling at Christmas time without partaking of the
hospitality of the place.

"The Colonel has asked me to send home with you a napkin of this-and-that from the table," the girl explained.

Nicolina and Sture protested against her generosity, but
nevertheless they were grateful for her offer. They would
now have something really fine to give to the Christmas elf.
"We'll put it in that reed basket we made at school before
Christmas," Nicolina suggested as she opened the napkin
and gasped at the beauty of the things knotted up in it.
There were five kinds of cookies and Yule kakar with frost-

ing in wiggly lines all over the top, and plum-bread with golden citron, and kringlor!

"Smell!" Nicolina breathed in delight. "Cinnamon!"

The best part of all was that they could now make a Christmas midnight supper for their mother. How wonderful it would be to have her home once more! Fru Ole's daughter was coming tonight, and once she had arrived they could have their mother back again.

The two fixed their gift for the Yule Nisse, then set about getting the Christmas supper ready. They put the branched red candlestick in the middle of the table. Blue candles went into it. Why, it almost looked like Christmas without another thing being added. However, when they had the fine food from the napkin, too, set out on the dishes, then it was indeed the Yule, and the two of them began singing "Silent Night, Holy Night."

They had just finished the last stanza when there was a knock on the door. Could it be that the Nisse had already found his basket there on the porch! They flung the door open and peered out eagerly. Someone stood there, but he was not the Yule Nisse.

"I've been on these skis since morning," said the stranger, "and I am tired. Might a poor sinner come inside and rest his weary bones by your fire for just a moment?

"Come inside, and a happy Christmas to you," said the two, as was the custom when someone came calling on this night. Then Nicolina added, "And sit, while I push the coffeepot upon the fire."

So while the stranger rested, Nicolina made him a pot of coffee, which filled the cottage with such fragrance that it smelled as though the Christmas celebrating had already started.

"We suppose," said Nicolina, "that you are on your way to visit your old father somewhere?"

"No," said the stranger, "I'm not, but how came you on such thoughts?"

Nicolina sighed. "Christmas is the time of year when the lost should return," said she. Then she glanced out the window toward the manor on the hill, where candles still blazed in the many windows. "Years ago," said she, "the man up there quarreled with his son. He wanted him to join the army and become a soldier like himself, but the boy did not want to be a soldier. He ran away to sea. The Colonel never hears from him any more, except for a letter that comes every Christmas."

"A letter?" the stranger asked.

"It comes from America," Sture answered, "but no one knows what is in it. The housekeeper believes that it comes from the son. But the letter never has any return address. In that way the Colonel can never write to his son and tell him how sorry he is because he was so unpleasant that the boy had to leave home."

"Is . . . is the Colonel well?" the stranger asked.

"No, he isn't well," Nicolina answered. "He has been in bed for years, and my mother says it is because the burden on his heart is so heavy that he has not strength enough to stand up under it."

"Perhaps you could go in place of the Colonel's son," Sture proposed, "and call on him this Christmas. It would help."

The stranger made circles on the floor with his ski-boot. "I wouldn't know how to act," said he, "and it has been so long . . . I wasn't prepared for anything like this tonight. I was on my way to Ski-valley, where I have old friends." It was as though the stranger were thinking out loud.

He went to the door and glanced off toward the big house on the hill. "I wouldn't know what to say. I'd be scared," he blurted out.

"We'll go with you," Nicolina offered, "and see to it that

you get let in without the old housekeeper scaring you."

"She is a sharp one. She has been with the Colonel since his son was a little boy. That is why the Colonel does not let her go, no matter how cross she gets," Sture explained.

The stranger said nothing on the trip over the glistening snow. The two children hurried as fast as they could lest the stranger change his mind and refuse to go on with the fine plan they had for him.

It was Sture who clanged the great bell above the door. He had meant to do the talking too, but it wasn't necessary. It was old Brita herself who came to the door tonight. "No, but it is you at last, Gunnard!" said she. "I dreamed last night that you were coming tonight, and that is why I have the candles lit. Your father is sitting up in his chair. He also was sure you were coming tonight."

The stranger stepped into the big hall. He removed his hat and looked about uncomfortably.

"I guess we can go back home now," Sture began, "so good night to you."

"No, don't leave me. Don't leave me yet!" the stranger begged almost sharply. So the two children followed him into the Colonel's room. The housekeeper's eyes were old. That was why she had thought this man was the Colonel's son, Nicolina and Sture were thinking to themselves.

The stranger paused in the doorway for a moment, then he gave a gasp of joy. "Father! Oh, father!" His voice broke then and he could say no more.

"Oh, my son," sobbed the Colonel, "I was afraid you would not come home in time for me to tell you how wrong I was!"

"You were right, Father, and I was wrong," replied Gunnard huskily.

"It was our prayers," said Brita, the housekeeper. "Twenty years of prayers make a mighty heap."

Nicolina and Sture slipped out quietly. "Did you ever see the like!" Nicolina whispered. "Gunnard, the lost son!"

As the brother and sister turned toward home in the moonlight it was as though they were walking on magic, for their own hearts had taken up full measure of the joy they had witnessed at the manor. The runners of their skis made pleasant songs as they skimmed over the snow's crust.

Their mother was at home and waiting for them. She had added to the good food on the table with contributions of her own. "Supper is ready, and a happy Christmas to us all!" said she.

Early Christmas morning they were out of bed and

dressed in their best clothes, for everyone in Sweden went to Yule-messa while it was still dark, on Christmas morning. Sture, Nicolina, and their mother were going to ride in the big sleigh coming from Thorsgard. It always had the finest flares and the best singers and the swiftest horses.

First of all Nicolina must rush outside, though, to learn whether or not the Yule elf had found his gift. It was gone. In its place were three immense packages, and they were tied with the same kind of golden ribbon as the Christmas elf had used for the packages under the Colonel's tree.

"To wish you as happy a Christmas as you have given me," was written on one of the tags, and it was signed "The Yule Nisse."

Nicolina and Sture sat down beside the chuggling coffee-pot and sighed in utter contentment. "How wonderful Christmas is!" they whispered, as they ran their fingers over the splendid tinsel ribbon that bound their beautiful boxes. It was a perfect Christmas, but they were thinking that it might have turned out very differently, had they not remembered to give a gift to the Yule Nisse.